The Mystery of Walla-Walla

By G. H. Teed

Illustrated by Val Reading

From **The Union Jack Library** magazine,
November 22, 1913. Series 2, No. 528.

Stillwoods Edition, 2020

Stillwoods.Blogspot.Ca

Catalogue Information:
Title: The Mystery of Walla-Walla
Author: G. H. Teed (1886-1938)
Illustrated by: Val Reading
First published in: The Union Jack Library magazine, November 22, 1913. Series 2, No. 528.
This Edition: Stillwoods, 2020 (Doug Frizzle)
ISBN Canada: 978-1-989788-11-0
Blog: Stillwoods.Blogspot.Ca
Author Blog: http://ghteed.blogspot.com/
Storefront: http://www.lulu.com/spotlight/lulubook22

Keywords: Sexton Blake, British fictional detective, Yvonne Cartier.

Yvonne Cartier visits her old homestead in Australia, to find that the present owner has been reduced to bankruptcy by his neighbour. She decides to assist him and at the same time to get vengeance on this neighbouring villain.

At the same time, Sexton Blake is enlisted by the neighbour to assist him in finding his lost stock. Sexton Blake and Tinker are put in danger!

Who is to win through? Can there be a justified solution?

CHRISTMAS DOUBLE NUMBER

"THE SACRED SPHERE"

This is the Title of Next Week's Special 80,000-word Yarn in the

"UNION JACK" LIBRARY

2d.

(See page 28.)

CHRISTMAS COMES BUT ONCE A YEAR,
AND WHEN IT COMES IT BRINGS GOOD CHEER

1913

The Mystery of
Walla-Walla

THE FIRST CHAPTER.   In the Grip of Drought—Despair — Yvonne Arrives at Her Old Home.

Australia lay parched and gasping in the grip of drought.

Thousands of square miles of what had been rich grazing country were now vast stretches of white, shrivelled grass, broken here and there by big patches of stiff red loam or hard packed "cement," from which the starved shoots had long ago disappeared. Over all hung the coating of sand which had been stirred up in the mallee country, and had come whipping across the land on the hot wings of the enervating north wind. The branches of the big blue-gum and box shade trees rustled monotonously with a slow, listless sweep.

Still whiter than the dead blue grass and salt weed, were the snowy corpses of heavily-woolled sheep, which had been beaten down in their battle against thirst, and had died where they lay, too weak to prolong the struggle. Here and there a little lamb bleated helplessly, gazing in surprised distress at the silent ewe, which for the first time had failed it.

Even the green shoots in the bottoms of the creeks and the bina-bongs had given out. The whole of the vast expanse presented a picture of panting, dying Nature.

For weeks had the drought continued. Day after day, long train-loads of stock had been hurried southwards, where, on the well-watered and green stretches of Gippsland they could exist until the drought broke, and the blessed rain came. But even then unnumbered thousands were left, and men, red-eyed from weeks of strained anxiety, gazed at the hot leaden sky with its brazen disc, and prayed or cursed as was their nature.

Not even the crops assisted in stemming the white flame of the drought. Great paddocks of wheat and oats, lucerne and ambercane had been scorched and shrivelled to hungry, weedy stalks. The grain lay in sickly tumbled heaps of whitened straw, the lucerne was burnt to brown, and the sap had long ago departed from the once juicy stems of the sorghum.

On the plains, where the vast network of irrigation channels assume the appearance of a giant spider's web, men fared better for a time. Then the channels had stopped their flow. Water was held back, and only dribbled out at ever-lengthening periods for stock purposes. The Murray and the Loddon had not been so low for years. The once bursting Lannecoorie Weir, with its enormous boosted capacity, was a tiny pond, with hardly enough to float a small rowboat.

Men, who had risked their all were forced to spend days and nights in the saddle, helpless to assuage the suffering, and forced to watch their stock dying in thousands, but still fighting, still hoping. Others, in desperation, dug countless pits in search of water.

Owing to the configuration of the country, the water table was not far down, and many cries of joy went up when, into the pits rushed that for which they sought. But what a cruel prank had Nature reserved for them. The water was brackish—unfit for man or beast, no matter how deadly was his need.

And throughout all this period of burning death, there were men who sought to benefit from the helplessness of their fellows; men who fought and cursed and drank; men who hung, ever watching, ever ready to snatch from the weaker grasp that which they coveted,

Binabong Station, once the richest stretch of land in the district, was not immune from the general blast of the drought. Since it had been the home of Mademoiselle Yvonne Cartier, the luxuriant paddocks and rich flats had fallen on evil times. Often had it changed hands since its prosperous days under the Cartier regime, and each time had something disappeared from its well-stocked equipment.

No more the great traction engine puff-puffed up and down the great paddocks, towing after it the little procession of disk ploughs and harrows; no more waved great stretches of wheat and oats; no more could be seen the rolling paddocks of rich fallow, and no more could be heard the cheery shouts of the stockmen and boundary riders, the jackeroo and roustabouts, or the sharp, excited bark of the shaggy sheep dogs as they careered madly around big molts of sheep to the resonant crack of the stock-whip.

Almost all its former bustle and life had disappeared. Only a few listless men remained, wrapped in the general air of desolation which overhung the place, and modelling their days after those of the owner.

Night was just giving way to the golden hue of dawn. The sun's disc rose like a ball of crimson, presaging still another day of hot, rainless horror. Up in the once beautifully furnished Binabong Station homestead sat the young owner, little heeding, the coming of another day.

In the slow creeping dawn-light his face looked drawn and haggard. Though barely thirty, he looked fifty. His eyes were puffed and swollen with the look one sees in those of a man who has caroused long and slept, little.

The now useless flame of the lamp which still burned, accentuated the drawn appearance of the man's face, and lent to the whole room a look of shame at being caught, as it were, by the pure brilliance of open day.

And well it might. If the man's appearance was dishevelled, that of the room itself was worse. On the table, at his ellow, stood two empty decanters, a half-filled syphon, and several glasses. The cloth was littered with cold butts of cigars, cigarettes and ashes. A few scattered cards lay about in the general disorder, while on the floor, where they had been carelessly thrown, were heaps upon heaps, presenting the appearance of a miniature snowfall.

Over all hung the heavy, stale odour of smoke and whisky. In the centre of this hideous array sat the man, his whole attitude that of complete despondency, of absolute and utter despair.

That was only one of many dawns during the drought which John Treherne had seen under similar surroundings. For six months he had fought the creeping scourge of drought, and fought gamely. Then the madness of it all had seized him. Like even stronger men than he, had he succumbed, and cursed blindly at the implacable decree of Nature. Unlike they, however, he had not given reign to his madness in a blind whirl of drunken revelry, from which they had emerged with shaking hands and lack lustre eyes, but still purged, and ready again to continue the soul-racking fight.

Better were it for John Treherne had he done so. Instead, he had fallen into toils as sinuous and as unyielding as those of the Evil One himself.

Two months before, his neighbour, the owner of the adjoining station of Walla-Walla, had come to him with offer of assistance— assistance for which John Treherne was duly grateful. This man, Edward Jameson, had then seemed like a helping hand sent by Providence itself. At first it had been the offer of a well-grassed paddock for some of Traherne's ewes which were lambing. Then had come the offer of another paddock for a mob of weaners. This, too, Treherne had accepted.

Why it was that Jameson was carrying no stock over all his great stretch of country he did not stop to ask himself. If only then he could have read the subtle cunning and diabolical cleverness of his "generous" neighbour.

Born in the country, bred in the bush, inured to the life of the back blocks, son of a shrewd, scheming father; who had risen from being a drover to the ownership of Walla-Walla, Jameson had cast a jealous eye at the rich acres of Binabong.

Long ago had his experienced eye seen the coming of the drought. Long ago had his fertile brain weaved its plans for clearing off his stock. This would achieve two ends at one stroke.

One was his own immunity from the effects of the drought, and the other was the reserve he needed in case Nature throw the winning cards into his hands. And with that almost uncanny encouragement which she seems to hand out to evil-doer, Nature had done just what he wished.

Patiently had he watched while his neighbours, Treherne among them, had hurried off their stock to Gippsland. From all over the country others were doing the same. Finally the word came that no more could be received. Gippsland was full. Even that rain-blessed region had its limits. Then did men tear the very thatching from their huts in a futile effort to save their stock. Then did John Treherne begin his long fight which had ended in ruin; and then did Edward Jameson play his first card.

In the guise of sympathetic friend had he ridden over to Binabong. Treherne was duly grateful for his offer, and seized on it with avidity. Two years only had he been out from England, and his life there had given him little opportunity of probing the depths and purposes of human nature.

Even the removal of the ewes and weaners had not availed— as Jameson, who had seen the full effect of a drought, knew it wouldn't. Then Treherne's stock had been paddocked near Jameson's boundaries. Jameson's well-stocked water tanks had been placed at his disposal. Only the huge overshot dam in Treherne's home paddock now served for Binabong's needs. The Binabong was empty; the creeks were dry.

Still the spectre of ruin stalked John Treherne, and then his wool company, who had been financing him until shearing should arrive, made demands. They must have money. He had none to give. Must he sell his sheep in order to realise? He had paid big prices for them in a booming market. Must he sacrifice them for the two and three shillings a head, which was all they would fetch in the glutted market of the present?

It seemed so, and yet, wait! There was one chance. Jameson had been more than neighbourly. He had been a godsend. He was wealthy, and, unlike most of the others, free from care. Perhaps he would help.

Acting on this thought, Treherne had ridden post-haste to Walla-Walla, and had besought Jameson's assistance.

How well he could remember his renewed hope as he rode back home with Jameson's promise of the amount he needed. How easy it had been. One word and his generous neighbour had said "yes"—with Treherne's stock as security.

In that mysterious way in which creditors seem endowed with a clairvoyant faculty, when a man is on his last legs, did others begin to press Treherne.

Nothing but money would do, and money they must have. They might as well have tried to squeeze blood from a stone, but still they persisted, and in his new extremity, Treherne turned once more to his neighbour; nor did he know that the same hand which helped him had been the same hand which had pressed him with his creditors.

After that he lived on grimly, but hopefully. The drought must break. His sheep were carrying heavy fleeces. His wool was clean, and would command good prices. Even through the drought had its "yoke" been apparent, a quality which had suffered in the fleeces of his neighbours' stock. His lambs would soon pick up, and their very pedigree would make them sought after by the "freezers."

But still that great brazen disc rise mockingly each day, and still the pit of ruin yawned. Every head of stock he owned was now pledged as security to Jameson. Yet he must have more money. To get it he must yield his last stronghold, the station itself, and that he had done.

His neighbour had come to his assistance, and though Treherne was the nominal owner of Binabong, Jameson was the practical owner. Still, if rain came, Treherne had a good fighting chance, and none knew it better than Edward Jameson.

It was then that his true cunning exhibited itself—a cunning which hastened its purpose, when his experienced eyes read signs of a change in the leaden dome overhead.

With Machiavellian duplicity, he himself grew despondent and gay by turns. One moment he would assert confidently that a change must come, and the next, with well-simulated gloom, he would sigh and shake his head dolefully at the inscrutable heavens.

By degrees the nerve-racked Treherne reflected his neighbour's moods, and when, with every nerve jagged from suspense, every fibre of his being shrieking aloud for some break in the awful monotony of waiting for the rain which never came, Jameson suggested a turn at the cards. Treherne agreed, grateful for the prospect of forgetfulness.

Night after night they played. At first it had been for small stakes, which Treherne always won. Then for larger, when Jameson's luck turned, and for a time they were about even. Then the nightly meetings became a regular habit. Certain hours were set apart. The stakes were again raised.

For days the north wind had been blowing with a heated ferocity which seemed to strain, with a terrible menace, at its bonds. It was not possible that such atmospheric conditions could continue without something snapping.

Treherne, now steeped in the fever of gambling, saw it not. Jameson watched its approach with a careful eye—and again the stakes were raised. For a week the play continued each night from dusk to dawn.

At the end of that time—the morning on which we see John Treherne sitting amidst the wreck of all his hopes—Jameson owned not only every head of stock which had belonged to Treherne, but he owned every solitary acre which went to make up that once magnificent estate, the pride of old John Cartier's heart, and the home of the incomparable Yvonne—Binabong.

Before, he had controlled them in that they were pledged to him. The coming break in the weather, however, had told him they might even then be snatched from his grasp. The parting feeling of ownership had been too sweet for Edward Jameson to relinquish easily, and so over the cards he had offered to play John Treherne for the debt on the sheep. If Treherne won he could take back every head without repaying a penny of the loan.

The younger man had jumped at the offer. They played, and Treherne lost. With seeming magnanimity, Jameson offered to repeat the offer, this time with the station itself as the stake. In his new despondency, Treherne took the bait.

Again they played. Again he lost.

Now Binabong and all its stock would pass to Edward Jameson in a transfer more binding than all the mortgages or deeds in existence, the transfer of honour.

And when Edward Jameson rode homewards, just before dawn that morning, he had a look of satisfied greed in his eyes, and an evil smile on his lips, which only passed away when the first faint streak appeared in the east.

He had played a long game, a patient game, a cunning game, and in his pocket he held the tiny slip of paper which gave to him all that which he had coveted, and beggared the man who had blindly trusted him of all his worldly possessions.

And yet on the hot wings of the parched dawn was coming to Edward Jameson a just and sweeping vengeance. Even as he cantered homewards through the spreading light, and even as John Treherne sat in huddled despair, reviewing his shattered past and his hopeless future, did the golden sun appear.

Barely had it risen like a great, crimson globe, floating in a sea of pink and gold, when against its brazen face were silhouetted two figures.

The early rising boundary-riders saw them far away over the rolling paddocks, and shrugged. Probably, only two more creditors hastening to snatch what they could, as many others had done during the past few weeks, they thought.

As the galloping figures drew nearer, however, they could make out that one was a woman. Her wide hat and regularly flapping divided skirt proclaimed her sex.

The other was a man. Truly a strange pair to arrive at Binabong so early in the morning.

Nearer and nearer they drew. Another strange thing. The woman took the lead, and rode confidently on, taking advantage of a short cut here, instinctively finding the best place to jump a creek there, riding, in fact, with an exhibition of knowledge regarding the best trail through the paddocks, which rivalled that of the oldest stockman.

His curiosity aroused, one of the younger jackeroos hailed old Gene, the head stockman, who had been on Binabong in its palmy days as well as through all its vicissitudes, and who had not yet appeared. In answer to the hail, however, he poked his grizzled head out of the bunk-house door, and demanded to know, in innocent profanity, what was wrong.

"I say, Gene, do come here and have a squint," called young Roberts, the jackeroo who had hailed.

The old stockman strode through the doorway, and leaping the drafting yard fence instead of going round it, cast his keen old eyes over the paddocks.

"What do you make of them?" queried Roberts. "There, you could see them quite plainly when they topped that rise. A man and a woman. Did you see how she led the way over that crab-hole stretch? Dash it all I've been on here over a year, and I never found that path myself until a week ego. Now they are coming to the creek. There, Gene, did you see that? Not a man on the place could have gone straighter for that narrow jump than she did. And by jingo, she's young, too. You can see her face now. They're strangers, that's a dead cert."

He broke off in his excited comments, and glanced at the old stockman, surprised that he had not been interrupted ere this by a profane command to shut up. His surprise changed to wonder as he looked, for old Gene was gazing over the paddocks with the alert expression of on old war-horse. His grizzled face seemed more weather-beaten than ever; his keen old eyes seemed suddenly filmed, and his gnarled hands were clenched tightly. He seemed oblivious to the presence of the other, as indeed he was. Then, suddenly his lips parted, and he spoke more to himself than to anyone else.

"There never weren't no female what knew those short cuts but the little missie," he said slowly. "I ain't never seen no one but the little missie put a horse along like that, and who should know better than me what taught her to ride."

"What on earth are you talking about?" asked the amazed jackeroo.

But old Gene was deaf to his question, and kept his eyes riveted on the rapidly approaching figures. Then he gave one great leap backwards, and tore at top speed for the bunk-house.

"Joe, Pete, Smith, Harris, Curly, Monty!" he yelled excitedly, dashing into the bunk-house. "Up, you lazy hounds, up quick! The little missie is coming."

Six pairs of booted feet struck the floor at the same moment, and six faces as grizzled as old Gene's peered in unbelief at the head stockman.

"Don't stand there like a lot of dummies!" he roared.

"Would you have the little missie come back without a welcome? She'll be here in a few moments."

"Are you crazy from the heat or is that on the level?" drawled Monty, though his twitching hands belied the calm of his manner.

Gene's subsequent profanity in lieu of an answer convinced Monty that it was "on the level," and then those six old veterans moved with alacrity. Six gnarled hands followed Gene's in dragging out heavy revolvers. With the smooth despatch born of long experience they filled every chamber. Then, with the head stockman in front, they contemptuously put aside the younger men who thought they had all suddenly gone mad, and, with old Gene leading, dashed out and across the drafting yards.

One long look did they take; one simultaneous gasp of surprised joy did they give as they saw the slim grace of the leading figure; then seven revolvers went up, and seven fingers emptied chamber after chamber on the morning air just as Yvonne, their "little missie," rode into the circle and sprang, half laughing, half sobbing with joy, into the welcoming embrace of those old veterans who had adored her from the cradle.

Many an old eye grew moist, and many a seamed face blushed with pleasure as her fresh young lips touched their weatherbeaten cheeks each in turn, and then what a wild, whole-souled cheer rent the air in joyous welcome to the "little missie."

"Oh, Gene, Monty, Smith, Harris, Joe, Pete, Curly," she cried, through her tears of happiness, "how good it is to see you all again! But what have you done to the dear old place? I could hardly believe I was on Binabong. But first, I want you to meet my uncle, Mr. Graves. Uncle"—and she turned to the smiling Graves— "come and shake hands with my dear old friends."

And then all tried to tell at once of the many girlish escapades of Yvonne when she had ridden through the great paddocks in joyous abandon, a stock whip in her hand and a shaggy sheep dog beside her. Once more she turned to old Gene and repeated her question.

"Well you might ask that, little missie," answered the stockman slowly. "Binabong ain't never been the same since you left. Me and the others would have left long ago only we ain't so young as we used to be, and changing goes hard. It has gone from bad to worse. First one thing and then another. When Mr. Treherne, the present owner, took it over we hoped for better things. He seemed to try and make something of it, missie, but I guess the drought and something else has about finished him."

"Something else, Gene!" said Yvonne quickly "What do you mean?"

"I means Jameson, missie."

"Ah, has he fallen into his hands?"

The old stockman nodded.

"I think so. Jameson has been here every day and every night for weeks. All the Binabong stock is on Walla-Walla, and if I know anything it is likely to stay there. I never did see Jameson or his father let go any thing they ever got their fingers on."

Yvonne nodded slowly.

"I know, Gene. He had his eye on Binabong after father died, only Ike Vineburg and his crew ruined us first and got it. I'm afraid uncle and I have come at a bad time, but I had such a longing to see the old place, Gene, I couldn't resist the desire."

"God bless you, little missie," exclaimed Gene, "me and the boys can't tell you how glad we are to see you again! We're only sorry, the place don't look like it used to. Will you stay long?"

"Well," laughed Yvonne, "we intended staying for a week or so, and were hoping to find agreeable people on the place. But if the present owner is in trouble he won't be very anxious to have strange guests about. Still, I think we will ride on to the house and see him. Perhaps you had better come, Gene, and tell him who we are. I'll see the rest of you later in the day," she added, turning to the other six. "Then we'll have one of our old gallops through the paddocks, though now there aren't any sheep to mob up," she finished, with a little catch in her throat.

"By heavens, missie, we'll get a mob of sheep for you to muster up if we have to take them at the point of the gun," drawled Monty, and his companions echoed his sentiments in no uncertain tones.

In the meantime Gene had saddled up a horse, and, waving her hand, Yvonne led the way to the house in a sweeping gallop.

Sitting in the room which formed the tomb of his dead hopes, John Treherne heard the sound of flying hoofs as they swept over the sun-baked ground towards the house.

"Good heavens!" he muttered bitterly. "Has Jameson brought his men to take possession already, or is it more of the carrion hanging about the corpse?"

He savagely kicked aside a fallen chair, and, getting stiffly to his feet, stumbled along the passage and out on to the verandah. There he stood blinking in the morning sun, his mind gradually coming from the abyss of his troubles to the fact that a delightfully, charming-looking girl and a middle-aged man in immaculate riding clothes were descending before him.

As his blood-shot eyes took in the vision of Yvonne's fresh beauty a slow, dull flush mounted over Treherne's features, and he half turned as though to seek the shelter of the house where the signs of his dissipation would be less visible.

Graves, man of the world as he was, sized up the situation in a glance. He had seen that heavy eye and that shaky hand too often not to be able to read their meaning. With a low word to Yvonne he went ahead with Gene, and held out his hand as the latter introduced him.

Talking casually he moved towards the door, and Treherne mechanically followed. Once out of sight of the girl Treherne recovered his composure and remembered his duties as host. Turning to Graves he said wearily:

"I'm very pleased, indeed, to meet you, Mr. Graves, but, to be perfectly frank, you come at a rather unfortunate time. To put it plainly, I am no longer the owner of Binabong. The ownership passed last night to my neighbour, Jameson, and I am practically only here on sufferance myself."

"Oh, that's all right!" drawled Graves cheerfully. "My niece used to own Binabong, and, as she was seized by a sudden desire to see it again, we came out from home with that intention. I'm sorry to hear that you are in trouble, and assure you we have no desire to intrude. However, you slip along and take a cold plunge. Then we'll breakfast together, and who knows, perhaps, we may be able to find some way out of your troubles,"

"That's impossible," answered Treherne gloomily, "but I'll act on your suggestion. Please make my apologies to your niece and tell her I shall receive her properly in half an hour. In the meantime, please make yourself at home. Your niece will know her way about as well as I"

"Right!" rejoined Graves.

As Treherne nodded and hastened away he turned to Gene.

"On the whole, I don't know but what our arrival was rather fortunate," he said, in low tones. "I've only seen that sort of a look in a man's eyes a few times, and each time it was when he had a sudden desire to gaze into the business end of a revolver with his finger on the trigger."

"You are not far wrong," answered Gene, gazing with new respect at Graves. "That look has been growing in his eyes for days. How Jameson has landed him I don't know, but I'll bet it wasn't on the square."

"Mr. Jameson evidently doesn't hold a very high place in your estimation," remarked Graves.

"You bet he doesn't," grunted the stockman. "Shall I bring in the little missie, sir?"

"Yes, you might."

Graves strolled along while Gene went to fetch Yvonne. By chance he stepped at the half-open door of the room where Treherne and Jameson had been gaming. With a grunt of disgust he strode across and threw open the window. Just as he had done so Yvonne entered, and stood looking in amazement at the scattered cards.

"So that is why our host wears such a look at sunrise," she murmured softly.

"And, if you ask me, that's how our host lost his station," replied Graves.

Yvonne's eyes clouded as she gazed at the scene of general disorder, and in her absorption she unconsciously bent and picked up several of the cards from the floor. These she absent-mindedly shuffled in her hands, her eyes looking at them unseeingly. Then as her thoughts came back to the present she glanced carelessly at their backs, taking in, as was her wont, the general details of the conventional design which adorned them.

Suddenly her hands stopped shuffling and her gaze grew steady. Puckering her face she bent lower, and for several minutes studied the design with some care. Graves, who had turned and was looking out of the window, did not see her stoop and quickly pick up several more from the floor. Once more she studied the designs and then she spoke.

"What is it I have always said you and your club cronies excel at more than anything else, uncle?" she asked, with apparent irrelevance.

Graves swung round quickly as he heard the curiously-strained note in her voice.

"Cards," he answered laconically. "Why?"

"Because you profess to know all about cards that there is to be known, and I wish your opinion on something."

"If it's worth anything you are welcome to it. What is it?"

12

"Will you examine the backs of these cards and tell me if you notice anything peculiar in the design?"

With surprise depicted on his countenance Graves strode across and took the cards which she held out. Then he took them closer to the window and began to examine them. For five minutes dead silence reigned. At the end of that time he turned slowly and their eyes met.

"By heavens, Yvonne," he breathed, "they are marked, every blessed one of them. It's cleverly done, too. None but the initiated could ever detect it."

Yvonne nodded.

"Yes, it was the curve of the scroll in the design which caught my attention. Mr. Blake explained it to me one time."

"Oh, indeed!" grinned Graves, as Yvonne blushed. "But Yvonne, this is serious," he added, more gravely. "If these are the cards with which Treherne and Jameson have been playing, one of them has been playing a crooked game."

"And from visible signs I would think it was not our host," remarked Yvonne. "At any rate, put some in your pocket, uncle. We may need them."

Graves had just managed to thrust those he held in his pocket when a footfall sounded in the passage outside and Treherne entered.

His face was still drawn and haggard-looking, and his eyes heavy, but he wore a much more presentable appearance and seemed more himself. He welcomed Yvonne courteously, and in a few moments they moved towards the breakfast-room.

Whether it was Graves's languid air of understanding or Yvonne's delicately-expressed sympathy it is hard to say, but, owing to one or both, before the repast was half over Treherne's story was falling in a torrent from his lips. Not a single detail did he miss.

From the time he had bought Binabong until he had, in his madness, risked its fertile acres over the cards he told his tale, and never did his hearers listen to a more heartbreaking story of struggle and setbacks, madness and despair, unless it were the story of Yvonne's own loss of the same station.

"I hope you won't think I am flinching from the result, mademoiselle," he said. "It is only now that I realise the whirl of madness in which I lived, and the realisation loses nothing of its bitterness that it comes too late."

"Certainly I don't think so," she replied. "By the way. Mr. Treherne, I'd like to ask you something about your gaming!"

"I will answer whatever you wish to ask."

"Did you or your guest supply the cards with which you played?"

"Why—er—let me see. If I remember rightly, I did at first until mine ran out. Then Jameson brought some with him when he came. In fact, now you mention it, I remember that, he supplied all we used lately."

"So I thought, Mr. Treherne," said Yvonne. "Since that is the case, I am going to show you something after breakfast which will startle you considerably, if I am not mistaken."

"What is it!" he asked, with a puzzled look.

"Let us not spoil this delicious breakfast by unpleasant details," laughed Yvonne.

But after breakfast she led the way back to the card-room, and there the stupefied John Treherne gazed in spell-bound amazement while Graves gave him his first lesson in marked cards. When Graves had finished, they adjourned to the cool sitting-room, where Yvonne had once had a memorable interview with two of the men who had brought financial ruin to herself and her mother. There she waved her companions to a seat, and, lighting a dainty cigarette, began to speak.

Slowly, and with soft, emphasis, she explained to John Treherne exactly who Edward Jameson was, and what he was.

Then she dwelt on her own loss of Binabong, and her great desire to return. From that she went to the subject of Treherne's troubles, and for another half hour spoke earnestly. At the end of that time Graves was smiling in languid enjoyment, and Treherne was gazing at her in undisguised admiration.

Silence reigned for some minutes after she had finished. It was broken by Treherne, who rose and held out his hand to Yvonne.

"Mademoiselle," he said slowly, "I feel that your advice is good. I place myself entirely in your hands."

"Then that is settled, Mr. Treherne," smiled Yvonne. "We will start this very day to arrange our little surprise for Mr. Edward Jameson, of Walla-Walla, and when we get through, well, we shall see what we shall see."

Yvonne is introduced to John Treherne, the ruined owner of Binabong Station. *(See page 5.)*

THE SECOND CHAPTER. Blake Goes to Australia— Jameson's Story—Blake Has a Desire to Read.

Some men are born to adventure, some man seek adventure, and some have adventure hurled at them from every point of the compass. In the latter category might be classed Sexton Blake, for, if any man ever lived in a continual round of danger and adventure, surely he is that man.

When he finally made up his mind to shelve professional duties and make a long-promised trip to Australia, where he had not been for some time, he made a menial vow that nothing would induce him to touch a case until his return. For a wonder Tinker heartily agreed with his master, and no more idle-looking pair could have been seen around Melbourne than Sexton Blake and his assistant, with their inseparable companion Pedro.

They were not known in Melbourne under those names, however. Blake rejoiced in the all-embracing name of Smith— without the "y" and the "e"—while Tinker posed fairly successfully as his younger brother.

Thus the "Smiths" came to Melbourne, bent on a quiet holiday, with perhaps a few races to liven up things, and thus did the Smiths get drawn into a strange whirl of adventure through no fault of their own.

The actual instrument which Fate chose to upset the detective's carefully formed plans came in the person of one Captain Brien O'Brien, late of His Majesty's Army, and one time study mate at varsity with Sexton Blake.

It was in the quietly elegant smoking-room at Menzie's Hotel that they met, and only a vigorous jab in the delighted captain's ribs kept that gentleman from blurting out Blake's name for all the world to hear. After he had decided to desist from using Blake's arm in a pump-handle, his incoherent exclamations gradually descended to intelligible English as approved by His Majesty's Government, and from the bombardment of questions Blake managed to grasp that his old pal "would be dashed if he didn't think this was the best thing that had happened since Adam was a yearling; yes, by gad!"

After that, Blake gathered that the captain desired to know "What he had been doing with himself, old dear? What had brought him to Australia? Was he married, and was this his son? (meaning Tinker).

Why was he incog?" and a dozen other whys, wheres, hows, and who's.

When the cyclone had somewhat subsided, Blake introduced Tinker, and, together, the three of them moved to a quiet corner of the smoking-room which looked out on Bourke Street.

While Blake and his old friend exchanged experiences of the years which had passed since they had come down from 'varsity. Tinker cast a contemptuous glance at Melbourne's prehistoric trams, which seemed to cling to that rising city like an "old man of the sea."

After some minutes a chance phrase caught his ear, and as it seemed to promise a change of some sort, he gave his attention to the conversation.

"But you must, Blake," the captain was saying. "Campbell is no end of a good sport, and he's got a topping place up country. Over a hundred thousand acres, all together, and, bad as the drought has been, he hasn't lost a sheep. All due to his artesian well, so he says. Anyway, I'm going up for a week or ten days. Tommy Morrison was coming with me, but he's off on aide duty to the governor, and cried off at the last minute. Campbell's younger brother is there, and you'll make a fourth for bridge. Now don't say no, old chap. Bring the lad along; you will be just as well off up there as here, and we'll have no end of a high old time."

"Campbell," remarked Blake musingly. "It wouldn't be old Dumpy Campbell, of Magdalen, would it?"

"Good heavens! yes," cried the captain, in delight. "I'd forgotten you and Dumpy used to be pals. Gad! now I remember the twenty-round go you and he had down behind the pub on Derby night. Scott! that seems an age ago!"

"Er—yes, Campbell and I used to be—er—good friends," put in Blake hastily, with a sidelong look at Tinker's grin as that sharp-witted young man gleefully drank in the reference to one of Blake's youthful escapades, a bit of information he would casually let drop some time in the future when Blake was wigging him for getting into a similar situation.

"Well, old man, what do you say?" persisted the captain. "Shall I wire Campbell that I am bringing you? Gad! he'll kill the fatted calf when he hears you are coming."

"All right," laughed Blake. "When do we start?"

"To-morrow morning. We will take the six-thirty-five from

Spencer Street, and go by way of Kerang. Campbell will have horses to meet us at Barham."

"That will suit me all right," answered Blake. "Mind, though, it's only for a week."

"Wait until we get you up there, old son," chuckled the delighted captain as he hastened away to send the wire.

•   •   •   •   •

Two evenings later, a party of joyous spirits sat down to dinner at the Campbell homestead. There was Campbell himself, a big, bluff, fair man, who had been fully as delighted at Blake's surprise visit as Captain O'Brien had prophesied; his younger brother, a miniature edition of the elder, who was swotting for the Indian Civil Service; Captain O'Brien, V.C., D.S.O., to give that high-spirited Irishman his full title; Sexton Blake, most entertaining and popular of companions; Tinker, who was still dazed at this new phase of his master, and lastly, Pedro, who had signalised his arrival by dealing out severe punishment to three sheep dogs, two greyhounds, and a German bearhound, thus winning his spurs in Australia, and at the same time the right to occupy the said bearhound's place in the dining-room, while that astonished canine sulked in the stables and nursed a jagged ear.

Just as they were sitting down, a loud clatter of hoofs sounded outside, and a moment later, a big, black-bearded man was ushered in by the Chinese house-boy.

Campbell greeted him courteously, but without warmth, and introduced him to the general company as Mr. Edward Jameson, a neighbour and owner of Walla-Walla Station, which adjoined his on the south side.

In deference to a request made by Blake on his arrival, Campbell introduced both him and Tinker under the name of Smith.

Then, in conformance with the unwritten law of bush hospitality, Jameson was invited to join the party, though, truth to tell, Blake, O'Brien, and their host would have preferred otherwise.

Any outsider, no matter how genial, was an intruder that evening, for the three old friends had many experiences to swop, and Tinker and the younger Campbell seemed to be hitting it off together in regular "fifty-fifty" style. However, there was nothing to do but accept the situation gracefully, and certainly, Jameson endeavoured to make himself agreeable enough.

As far as Campbell was concerned he neither liked nor disliked his neighbour. He himself was one of those men who make few friends in later life, preferring rather to stick to those of his youth. Of a cold, reserved manner to strangers, he was warm enough to his old school friends. Although he was neighbourly enough with Jameson, it had never entered his head to become intimate with the man. In thought, in tastes, in everything they were as far apart as the poles, and at that Campbell had dismissed the matter from his mind.

Those who knew Jameson, and knew his nature, dealt with him accordingly. In a land where sharp practice upon the new chum is looked upon as good business (as indeed it is in most new countries), Jameson was by no means considered the heavy villain of melodrama. He was reputed one of the shrewdest stockmen and sharpest business men in the state, and if he ever did do anything flagrantly over the odds, no one knew it but Edward Jameson.

There were old drovers who remembered when his father had "humped a swag" (tramped) through the bush before a stroke of luck and a colossal nerve had started him on the road to success, or, at least, to what the world calls success.

Edward Jameson was a worthy product of his sire, and this was the man whom, for the first time, Sexton Blake met that night. How little did it occur to any one of them that ere long they were to be mixed up in a seething cauldron of intrigue, where every elemental passion of the bush was to be let loose.

For the first half hour the sole topic of conversation was the drought which had scared the country with its scorching breath, and which had not yet broken.

From that the talk veered to the Yellow Peril, and then onto the old days of the gold rush and the bushranger—the latter probably as fascinating a subject for conversation and conjecture as it is possible to find. Many and weird were the tales which went the rounds at that table, until, when the coffee was brought in and the servant withdrew, the bushranger reminiscences held first place.

And well they might, for in that very district had the famous Captain Starlight and his gang spread terror and death.

"I was reading in an old book the other day all about this district during the reign of the bushrangers," remarked Campbell, during a lull in the conversation. "It is a little known fact that when Starlight transferred his energies in the direction of Oodnadatta he left behind a lieutenant, who kept up the game here. In that article I came across a most interesting thing."

"What was it?" asked O'Brien.

"I'll tell you. It seems that this lieutenant, his name was Jackson, did things on a greater scale even than his old chief, Captain Starlight. Where the captain had confined himself to robbing the gold transporters and taking a few horses now and then, Jackson went in for wholesale sheep and cattle rustling.

"This district, in those days, was held by just one or two men, who had enormous mobs of stock grazing over it. After branding, they sometimes didn't see those same cattle for a couple of years. For a man of Jackson's daring this formed a tempting opportunity, which he evidently couldn't see pass. At any rate, he and his gang began rustling off big mobs of sheep and cattle from the outside edge of the run.

"The stockmen knew this was being done, and they felt pretty certain Jackson was the one who was doing it. Time after time they set out to catch him, but always failed. More than once they kept their eye on a special mob, and waited for their man to turn up. He invariably did so, and from under their very noses took the mob.

"Now, you all know, a man can pick up a coin or a ring and stand a pretty fair chance of getting away with it. But when it comes to making a clean bolt over several hundred miles of bush country with two or three hundred head of cattle, well, it seems ridiculous. Evidently the stockmen of those days thought so, for they lost no time in getting after Jackson. A few hundred head of cattle leave a trail behind that a blind man could follow, and yet, do you know, that not once were they able to follow Jackson. They kept track of him easily enough for a certain number of miles, and then they lost him absolutely. It was as though he and the cattle had completely vanished into the air, and yet they knew he hadn't, for about six months later they would hear that some cattle had been sold in Adelaide, whose brands looked mightily as though they had been changed.

"Where they had disappeared to, and how they had reached Adelaide was a mystery, nor has it ever been found out to this day. Now, you brainy gentlemen, there is the riddle, how did Jackson manage to practically evaporate with two or three hundred head of stock, not once but dozens of times?"

As he finished speaking Campbell re-lit his cigar and leaned back. If he had expected to interest his guests he had certainly managed to do so. Each one showed his interest in his own way. Captain O'Brien's eyes sparkled with a tactician's appreciation of Jackson's cleverness; Blake's eyes rested thoughtfully on the table; Tinker still gazed in fascination at the narrator; the younger Campbell had something of the same look; but Jameson wore the oddest expression of all.

He was leaning forward with one elbow on the table, and one great fist pressing into his bushy black beard. He was gazing at Campbell, and his eyes held a strange, tense look in them. Before anyone else broke the silence, his clenched fist dropped heavily to the table and he spoke.

"I heard that same yarn about Jackson from my father," he said, in full, deep tones. "I guess it's true enough too, but by heavens! I can tell you a stranger tale than that, and it didn't happen fifty years ago neither. It happened just this past week, and for all I know may even be happening at this very moment."

They all glanced at him in surprise. His tones were not those of the dinner table, and his manner held a hint of deadly calm, strangely at variance with the festive array.

"What on earth is it?" blurted out the captain. "By gad, Mr. Jameson, you have aroused my curiosity."

"Let us have it," said Campbell quietly. "If it can beat that tale of Jackson it must be worth hearing."

"I'll tell it," replied Jameson, "and let me say before I begin, that it is so true, there is a standing offer of one thousand pounds to the man who can explain it. It has to do with stock, and it has to do with their disappearance. Moreover, those are not the only joints on which it runs parallel to the Jackson yarn.

"Two weeks ago, my stockmen split up all the sheep on my place into small mobs, and spread them over the paddocks in order to equalise the food."

"Why, I thought you cleared off all your stock before the drought came," interrupted Campbell in surprise.

The silent "Mr. Smith" was the only one who saw a lightning look flash in and out of Jameson's eyes as he answered:

"So I did, but I took over Treherne's stock a short time ago."

"Oh! I beg pardon," rejoined Campbell, "Go ahead!"

"As I was saying," went on Jameson. "I gave orders to split up the stock. This was done, and owing to the continuance of the drought every mob, even those in the far paddocks, was inspected daily. Just a week ago, I was sitting down to breakfast, when one of the stockmen rode up and informed me that a small mob of about four hundred cross-bred ewes could not be located. Cross-breds are the very deuce as you know for going through fences, and, thinking this had occurred, I sent him back with instructions to muster up all the sheep in the near-by paddocks, and see if they had got mixed up. It wouldn't have been hard to tell, for the cross-bred ewes were a separate lot and everyone had a blue raddle mark on the back.

"Later in the day, the head stockman himself turned up, and reported that they had searched high and low, but could find not the slightest trace of the ewes. Naturally, I cursed him out for a chuckle-headed idiot, but he still persisted in saying he had had the paddocks scoured, so I arranged to look into the matter myself on the following morning. Well, after breakfast I was just about to start out when one of the men rode up and said that some three hundred wethers, which had been in a small paddock by themselves, had disappeared overnight.

"Things began to look serious, but several hundred sheep couldn't get far without someone seeing them, and as far as I knew they hadn't acquired wings. I thought they must have worked through the fences, and made back to Treherne's station. When another clean sweep of my own paddocks gave no sign of them I felt certain this must be the case. Consequently my head stockman and I rode over and investigated.

"Treherne, who has visitors, told me I was welcome to search, which I did. All his men turned out too, and it didn't take me long to discover that there wasn't a single head of live stock, bar the horses, on his place. It was impossible for them to get over to your place Campbell, for the river would prevent that."

Campbell nodded.

"Certainly," he said briefly.

"That was five days ago," resumed Jameson. "The morning after that one of the men reported that another four hundred ewes had disappeared. Things began to look serious with a vengeance, I can tell you. Hot on top of that information I sent nearly every man on the place riding across the country to spread the news.

"They went in every direction, and notified everybody. If they had been rustled off the place there was only one way for the thieves to get them away, and that was by the old stock road which cuts through this district, and runs clear on to Queensland. My men traversed that road for sixty miles each way, and nary a sign of sheep or drover did they see.

"That night I sent the few men who remained on the place to ride the paddocks and keep watch. They did so, and yet, when morning came, they found not only another five hundred wethers missing, but one of my men had disappeared as well. Taking that as a definite start we worked in every direction. Giving the thieves the very limit, they hadn't many hours' start, and as you know sheep travel slow, particularly in this kind of weather. It seemed a most certainty that we would overtake them in a couple of hours.

"Just, as we started out we met the others returning with the news of their unsuccessful journey and they joined us. We all knew every foot of the country, and yet, will you believe it, we scanned every mile of it within a radius of forty miles, and not the barest sign did we see of the missing sheep."

"Gad!" muttered the Captain. "This beats old Jackson, the bushranger, to a frazzle."

"I thought perhaps the missing man had gone after them," went on Jameson, not heeding the interruption, "but when we got back he and his horse were still missing. Tired as we all were we kept a close watch that night. Nothing happened, so leaving the men to do day duty in watches we got some rest.

"That afternoon in broad daylight two hundred weaners disappeared from a far paddock, and the search began again.

"Once more we covered every foot of Treherne's place. I could not get it out of my head that they had worked through the boundary fence, and had spread out over his scrub land, it was useless, however. Still we heard no news of the missing man, but that night—that was the night before last—his horse trotted home alone.

"Where he had been or where he had just come from, we couldn't imagine. He was as fresh as could be, and neither hungry nor thirsty. Nothing more happened until last night.

"As usual we were keeping a close watch, but from the only place where the guard was slack another hundred disappeared. You know one man on a good horse can patrol a big stretch of country by day, but when it is dark, it would take five times the number of men I have to keep a proper watch over my place.

"All day to-day we have been scouring the country high and low, without any success. It seems a strange coincidence that you should tell that Jackson yarn, Campbell, for it was to seek assistance that I really rode over tonight. That, gentlemen, is the yarn, and I think you will agree with me that it caps the bushranger's tale."

Then suddenly, before Campbell had a chance to reply, the quiet voice of "Mr. Smith" broke in.

"I make it some nineteen hundred sheep have apparently vanished from your paddocks into thin air," he said.

"Roughly that," answered Jameson.

"Mr. Smith" relapsed again into silence, and Campbell took up the conversation.

"Well, I certainly must acknowledge that your story is one of the most remarkable that I ever heard," he said. "It seems utterly inconceivable that nearly two thousand sheep and an able-bodied man could vanish in such a manner. As you say, there is only one way by which they could be driven out of this district, and that is by the old stock road."

"And I'll wager a hundred to one, they did not go that way." broke in Jameson. "My men searched it too carefully."

"Of course," remarked Campbell. "They couldn't get them half a mile along there without some boundary rider spotting them."

"I don't know of a single thing we haven't already investigated," said Jameson gloomily. "Every surrounding station has been searched or interviewed; boundary riders questioned; drovers cross-examined; every track and trail investigated by the boys. I tell you, say what you will, there is something mighty queer and uncanny in the way those sheep have vanished. If it were wet weather we would stand a better chance of following them, but even without that, it is hard to see where they have gone.

"Why, even supposing the rustlers managed to get the first lot or two safely away before we began our search, it would be physically impossible for them to get the other lots beyond the radius of our investigations.

"By all the laws it seems out of the question that the sheep can be far away, and yet every mile of country has been gone over. At any rate, I want the loan of a few of your men, Campbell, if you can spare them, and whoever solves the riddle gets a thousand in hard cash."

"I imagine they will jump at the chance," answered Campbell. "Of course, you are quite welcome to their assistance. I'll arrange with the head stockman to take half of them, and go over to-night. In the morning they can return, and the other half under the assistant stockman can then go over."

"I say, Campbell," broke in the irrepressible captain. "It seems to me Mr. Jameson's mysterious loss offers a topping chance for excitement. What's the matter with us taking a hand in the search. I'm sure it would appeal to Smith. That is, if Mr. Jameson has no objection."

Campbell glanced inquiringly at Blake,

"What, do you say, Smith?" he smiled. "Would it appeal to you?"

The quiet "Mr. Smith" disregarded a blatant look from Tinker as he knocked the ash from his cigar.

"Well, I don't know, old man." he replied. "If the situation is as Mr. Jameson outlines, it seems to me that it should be a very fascinating riddle to solve."

"I'm sure I should appreciate your assistance immensely, gentlemen," said Jameson rising. Then, turning to his host, he added:

"If you will excuse me now, I shall he getting along. I suppose it will be all right if I tell your head stockman you wish to see him?"

"Oh, yes, indeed, but I'll come along with you and arrange matters at once."

When Campbell and Jameson had disappeared in the direction of the front door, the others launched out into an animated discussion of Jameson's strange tale. Even though the old bushranger story was adorned with all the trappings of romance which fifty years had added to if they one and all confessed that Jameson's tale had it beaten to a frazzle, to use the captain's favourite expression.

It seemed endowed with all the spirit of adventure of an adventurous bush; it had the real tang of buccaneers, and they of no mean order, judging from their activities during the past week; and its very incongruity with known conditions lent to it a fascination which made even Blake's hardened pulses quicken a trifle.

As for Tinker, he was already forming half a dozen theories which might explain the remarkable disappearance of the sheep. And be sure the mystery lost none of its attraction in the contemplation of Jameson's remark, that, even while he sat there telling them of it, another mob might be going the way of the others.

The fact that one of his men had also disappeared stamped the affair with deep purpose, which could not be denied, and the inexplicable return of his horse, riderless and still fresh, endowed that particular incident with sinister meaning.

Where were the sheep? Where was the missing man? What could possibly have become of them? And above all, why—why—why? Why was Jameson made the sole recipient of the attentions of the mysterious stock-rustlers? What did it presage, and behind all his outward frankness had he any real notion of the motive, and any suspicion of the perpetrators?

Though some of these questions were openly voiced, they were all being turned over and over in the analytical mind of Sexton Blake. He was still pondering over the many points which were naturally presented, when the captain, who had been talking enthusiastically with the younger Campbell and Tinker, turned to him and remarked:

"By jingo, old man, I don't know how this thing strikes you, but it has gripped me harder than anything since I read 'Treasure Island.'"

Blake smiled. The captain's enthusiasm took him back to his younger days, to that door which "once you leave its portals you can ne'er return again"—his schooldays.

"I must, confess it does attract me," he said, "but perhaps Mr. Jameson is painting the thing too luridly. If it were as he says, we would be in the position of trying to believe some two thousand sheep and an able-bodied man had vanished into thin air, not to mention the horse, which evidently returned to earth unharmed after its experiment in aviation. I imagine we shall find the whole thing capable of a very simple explanation, and Jameson will see his sheep trotting home bringing all their tails behind them."

"But, guv'nor," broke in Tinker eagerly, "there's one thing which makes it seem pretty real."

"What's that, my lad?" drawled Blake.

"Why, the fact that the drought is on and feed is scarce. They can't live without grass, and surely two thousand sheep couldn't wander about, at a time when every acre is precious, without someone seeing them!"

"True, my lad," laughed Blake. "That is exactly why I maintain that the thing is capable of a very simple explanation."

And only then did Tinker see that Blake had made his remark, not necessarily because he himself believed it, but because he wished to spur the others into advancing theories from which his keen mind might pick a germ of wisdom.

Just as he finished speaking their host returned, and they all noticed that he wore a serious look. He resumed his seat in silence, and after lighting a fresh cigar, turned to Blake.

"This ought to be somewhat in your line," he remarked slowly.

"Just what I said!" chuckled the captain.

"Well," went on Campbell, after a tolerant smile at the irrepressible one, "Jameson told me a few details outside which he didn't care to go into here, but gave me permission to tell you if I wished."

"Ah!" remarked Blake. "That is what I was hoping for."

"It seems," continued his host, "that for some reason or other he suspects his neighbour Treherne of having a hand in the business. Why, I don't know. It seems that all through the drought he has financed Treherne, and has saved him from ruin. The sheep which are on Walla-Walla were partial security for the money advanced, and he held a mortgage on Binabong Station itself for the balance."

"I beg your pardon," interrupted Blake quickly. "What is the name of Treherne's property?"

"Binabong," answered Campbell. "Why?"

"Did it used to belong to one Cartier—John Cartier?"

"Yes; but that was some years ago."

"I know. Go on, please."

"A week ago," resumed Campbell, "Treherne was absolutely and completely broke—or so Jameson says. In fact, Jameson went over one night, and from what he said I gathered that Treherne practically made a complete assignment of the property to him. Then, the very next day, he turned up with sufficient money to redeem the mortgage on the place.

"This Jameson refused to accept, on the grounds that he holds Treherne's written assignment of the property. Treherne has visitors there, and Jameson's theory is that they must have advanced the money. At any rate, that left a deadlock between them. Jameson claims the station as his property, and Treherne refuses to give up possession."

"The law would soon settle the question of ownership," remarked the younger Campbell.

"For some reason, Jameson wishes to avoid litigation," rejoined his brother. "Anyway, it was on the very day after his interview with Treherne that the first mob disappeared. I have met Treherne several times, and though I know he has been drinking a bit lately, owing to worry, I always thought him a very decent sort, and I can't conceive that he would do anything crooked.

"However, that is not all. When Jameson told me as much as he did, I thought, it permissible to take a liberty. I hope you won't mind, Blake, but I told him your real name. He at once asked me to use my influence with you to try to persuade you to bring your powers to bear on the matter, and I told him I would. Personally—and I think the rest of you are the same —the thing attracts me marvellously. He is prepared to pay well for your services."

"I don't mind looking into it," answered Blake, after a short pause. "Of course, reimbursement is quite out of the question. I am out here for rest and pleasure, nothing else. At the same time, if we join in and help Jameson, it will give us some excuse for keeping in the saddle, if nothing else, and I think that will not do us any harm. Therefore, Campbell, on the distinct understanding that my identity does not go past Jameson, I am willing to give my assistance for what it is worth."

"Hooroo! Hooray!" cried the captain. "And now, what is the general opinion on starting this very night?"

"I say yes," replied the younger Campbell, Tinker, Captain O'Brien, all in one breath.

"What do you say, Blake?"

"Well," smiled the latter, "it might be as well if some of us rode over with your men and took a hand. Since this bloodthirsty trio seem so keen on it, suppose they go? Then the captain could take proper charge of your men. As for you and myself—I suggest that we remain at home and play a hundred up at billiards."

"All right."

Barely had Campbell said the word when the captain, Tinker, and Campbell's brother rose and prepared for their departure.

Campbell rang and sent the Chinese boy with orders to have horses saddled up. Blake remained seated at the table, puffing thoughtfully at his cigar, and absently drumming on the arm of his chair with his long, sensitive fingers. Ten minutes later the three horsemen departed, to the accompaniment of a clatter of hoofs; and Campbell, who had been seeing them off, returned to the dining-room and sat down again.

"Well, old man," he finally remarked, "don't you think this affair peculiar?"

Blake nodded.

"Yes," he said slowly. "To tell you the truth, Dumpy, I intend taking it on, and endeavouring to ferret out the mystery; but not for five minutes would I pledge my unreserved services to Jameson without knowing more of the details. If he suspects his neighbour Treherne, he must have stronger grounds for doing so than he told you; for, unless Treherne were an arrant fool, he would never risk stealing a few hundred head of sheep over a land dispute of such magnitude. If he did it would ruin his case before any judge."

"By Jove, I believe you're right, Blake! But let us forget it for to-night. How about that game of billiards?"

"I've changed my mind," smiled Blake. "If you don't mind, I think I shall retire early, but before doing so I'd like to have that book about Jackson, the bushranger. I have a consuming curiosity to read it."

And as his host went to get it, he never for one moment dreamed that Blake's request had even the remotest connection with the mysterious disappearance of Jameson's sheep.

Gone, after throwing Tinker roughly down, advises
him not to try any games.

THE THIRD CHAPTER.   The Sheep Stealers —Tinker Captured— His Escape.

"S-h!"

The low, sibilant sound floated gently through the night. So faint was it that it seemed to blend with the soft rustling of the leaves in the surrounding trees.

The hot Australian night was but a black replica of the day just gone. Overhead the stars glittered strangely bright in their sea of indigo. The purple dome appeared to be pressing down with implacable force upon gasping Nature. From far away came the low neighing of a horse; somewhere in the distance could be heard the plaintive bleat of a thirst-maddened sheep; nearer at hand came the unmistakable odour of cattle; while over all hung the dusty, pungent, alluring smell of the stock-route and paddocks.

It was a true bush night, one of those nights when men beyond the outposts of the empire lay on their backs with memories of home and friends blending with the hot, earthy smell of the paddocks.

"S-sh!"

Again the sibilant sound floated out on the night breeze, and this time it was followed almost at once by the soft crushing of bushes, as first, one mounted figure, then another and another, rode quietly out from a dark patch of scrub, and drew up their horses beneath a big gum tree.

There were ten in all, and when the last horse had been drawn up in the shadow, the first figure which had ridden forth detached itself from the group and rode out a short distance. There it stopped, and for five minutes horse and rider were motionless as a statue. At the end of that time it turned and rode back to the group.

Could a light have been cast on the mysterious party which seemed so intent on keeping their movements quiet, it could have been seen that the figure which appeared to take the leadership was that of a woman, and that her features were those of the charming girl who was visiting Binabong. Nor would one have been mistaken, for it was none other than Mademoiselle Yvonne.

Edward Jameson was not far wrong when he suspected the mysterious disappearance of his sheep as emanating from Binabong; and yet though he felt vaguely that this was so, his several sweeping searches over that station had yielded not the faintest item whereby he might pin his suspicions to solid fact. A thing which is not surprising, for Mademoiselle Yvonne's bronze-crowned head had cooked up a most baffling plot against Edward Jameson, and under her slim hands the baking was being done to perfection.

It was true that from Treherne's visitors had come the money which he had offered to redeem the mortgage on Binabong. Had the owner of Walla-Walla been as cautious as his reputation proclaimed, he would have accepted this money, wondered as he might, and set it down to an unexplained failure. But old Gene, the head stockman on Binabong, had not been far wrong when he said once the Jamesons got their hands on a thing they found it hard to let go. It was exactly this, the sweet feeling of possession, which had blinded Jameson's clear judgment of details.

Never for a moment did he connect Treherne's repudiation of his assignment over the gambling to aught but a refusal to meet his obligations of honour. The fact, that the marked cards might have been spotted did not enter his head. He felt quite confident that long ere this they had been swept up by the servant, and burned.

Had he only possessed the faintest inkling of the identity of Treherne's guests he would have found therein some considerable shock to his hardened nerves. He did not know this, however, and consequently he railed in futile anger at the baffling and mysterious disappearance of mob after mob of sheep.

To those who have no intimate knowledge of the bush, it might seem that large lots of sheep could not be spirited away without leaving a broad trail behind them. That is quite true—and had there not been several months of drought, Yvonne's plans would have been impossible to carry out.

The months of burning rainless conditions, however, had packed the ground as hard as cement. And this ground still retained the crossing and re-crossing tracks of mobs of sheep over a long period of time.

Consequently, when Jameson's mobs were spirited away, they were sent over this criss-crossed land into a maze of tracks which the cleverest stockman found impossible to decipher.

But that did not explain where they now were, nor would that riddle be read for some time. That was Yvonne's secret, and well had she guarded it for many years.

The nine figures which she approached lounged easily in their saddles awaiting her orders. Old Gene was at one end of the line and Graves at the other. Between them were Treherne, Monty, Pete, Joe, and the rest of the old veterans who had met Yvonne with such a whirlwind greeting on her return to Binabong.

Nine grim, determined, hardened horsemen, seven of whom, at least, were as much at home in the bush at night as the average Londoner in Piccadilly. Nine armed, mounted men, each and all of whom answered in perfect accord to the orders of the slim girl who sat her horse with such perfect ease.

Presently she spoke.

"Gene!" she hardly breathed.

"Yes, missie?" whispered back the stockman.

"You take Monty and Pete with you. Circle around until you come to the far gate in the lower paddock. Joe and Smith will come with me. We will circle in the opposite direction. You, uncle, with Mr. Treherne, and the others, ride straight for the gate. Whoever gets there first do nothing but wait for the others. In that way we can get an idea as to where Jameson's guards are to-night. We shall make an attempt to get that small mob of wethers in the lower paddock. Now, ready—ride!"

Silently, nine figures swung and sought their respective places. Then, at a further command, they broke off into three parties, and stole off like silent shadows through the night, the muffled hoofs of the horses making no sound on the hard ground.

As they parted and rode forward each one loosened the heavy revolver in his belt, and took a firmer grip of the long, snake-like stock-whip which was coiled about his free arm, Jackson, the bushranger, and his companions never conceived a more daring raid, nor did they ever carry it out with more practised stealth than did Yvonne and her companions that night.

Well she knew that Jameson was not the man to take his losses lying down, and well she knew every man he could command would be on guard that night. Gene and his grizzled companions had brought in news regularly of how the owner of Walla-Walla and his men were scouring the ranges for miles in an endeavour to locate the missing sheep. With many chuckles of delight did the old stockman tell of the futile search over Binabong and the repeated questioning of boundary riders and owners.

In order to ensure secrecy and guard against betrayal, Treherne, at Yvonne's suggestion, had let go all his men, with the exception of Gene and his companions. Owing to the fact that Binabong was denuded of stock, and everybody expected to hear of Treherne's ruin any day, this had been accomplished without arousing any suspicion in the minds of the men concerned. Then Yvonne had called around her the loyal old fellows who had fared so well when the Cartiers owned Binabong, and to them had propounded her plan.

Not since he had ridden the ranges down by the Rio Grande and had lived in the cattle atmosphere of old Texas and Arizona had Gene been so delighted.

With Joe and Smith riding silently on either side of her, Yvonne began circling around towards the rendezvous, with all the caution of a born scout. Through great stretches of treeless paddocks she rode, over dried-up streams, and into black patches of scrub where the swish, swish of the branches against the horses' flanks gave the only indication that the shadows concealed moving life. Then along through a gaunt-looking expanse of ring-barked country until she reached the boundary fences dividing Binabong from Walla-Walla.

Even as the trio of riders reached this did Joe's keen ears detect the pad, pad, pad of a horse with unmuffled hoofs, and with one accord Yvonne and her companions rode silently into the shadow of a big gum tree.

Barely had they gained the safety of this retreat, when the sound they had heard increased, and silhouetted against the studded heavens they made out the figures of two horsemen cantering by on Jameson's side of the boundary fence.

"Our friend is risking nothing to-night." breathed Yvonne, when the riders had disappeared into a patch of scrub. "But come, we will need all our caution."

At her word they moved on again, keeping close to the fence.

For a full half-hour they rode on in dead silence, until they reached a cluster of gum trees, from which came the soft hoot of an owl. This, the prearranged signal, meant both the other parties had arrived. Gene and his companions had seen three of Jameson's men riding past; but Graves and Treherne, who had come direct through the Binabong paddocks, had seen or heard nothing.

"Even if he suspects that the sheep are disappearing in the direction of Binabong he is bound to have guards all round his boundaries," whispered Yvonne. "At the same time, he may have on an extra force, so move cautiously, and keep your ears and eyes open. Slip on ahead and open the gate. Gene."

The stockman rode on ahead, followed by the others. He stopped in the corner formed by the boundary fence and a sub-divisional fence, and after a few moments' manipulation at the high, skeleton-looking cyclone gate swung it back on its hinges, and the party rode through.

"Where did you see the sheep at sundown?" whispered Yvonne.

"Up here to the left, missie," answered Gene. "They were mobbing up for the night right near the boundary fence."

"Then lead the way, Gene, and we will follow. One of Jameson's men is bound to be not very far away from them, so move quietly."

Following Gene, they rode on silently through Jameson's paddock, keeping close to the fence. Then suddenly Gene drew up, and as the others approached they could see against the ground a large number of shadowy white blotches like so many kneeling Arabs at prayer.

There was no need for instructions then. Each man knew what he had to do. Spreading out as only experienced stockmen can, they circled the mob of sheep, which lay in a bunch, as is their habit, and when they had gained the far side brought into play the stock-whips which all this time they had carried.

With a good sheep dog to spur on a mob of sheep it is a comparatively easy matter for one man to drive a large number when he has the light of day to guide him and has not the need to work in silence; but at night, when a voice must not be raised, when a dog must not be used, and when a stock-whip must be flicked about their legs, but not "cracked," it is no easy matter, even though the number of the sheep be small and those who are driving them numerous and experienced. However, Yvonne and her companions had done it before, and they intended doing it again.

While half of them dismounted and, with bridle-reins trailing over their arms, went in amongst the startled sheep to rouse them, the other half went to work at the rear, flicking gently but persistently with their stock-whips, until the recumbent animals rose and crowded on against those in front.

Then the men amongst the sheep made their way out. Mounting, they spread out along the flank on the far side from the boundary fence. Gene and his half kept working in the rear; the boundary fence itself formed a barrier on the other flank. The silent, persistent, irritating flick at their legs kept the sheep on the move, and perforce they moved in the only direction which was possible—ahead.

On they went in this fashion until the leaders, who had been rubbing against the fence, felt a sudden end to this barricade, while in front appeared a new obstacle in the form of the sub-divisional fence. Forced on by those behind, they took, as always, the line of least resistance, and poured through the gate into the paddock belonging to Binabong—the same gate through which they had gone to Walla-Walla when Treherne had first fallen into Jameson's web.

The last one through, Yvonne and her companions closed up and followed. Gene was behind, and just about to close the gate, when a soft pad, pad sounded, and the dark silhouette of a flying horseman appeared. Without pausing, he rode on recklessly to within a few feet of the silent party, and even in the starlight could be seen the steely glint of his revolver as he threw it up and cried out:

"Hands up—quick!"

"What for, mister?" drawled Gene, riding forward, and followed at a short distance by Yvonne.

"For sheep stealing," came the steady voice from behind the gun. "Put them up, I say, and keep them away from your belt."

Old Gene obediently raised his hands, but pressing with his knees still guided his horse onwards until its flank and that of the newcomer's horse were pressing against one another.

"What will I do now, mister?" asked old Gene softly; while from Yvonne came a soft laugh.

"Do you expect to shoot us all?" she asked.

"No; I can see you are too many for one," came the quick retort. "But I can get help and overtake you before you get far with those sheep."

With that, the speaker lowered his revolver and jerked at his rein, intending to turn and ride for help. He counted without one thing, however, and that was the presence at his side of one of the most experienced and canniest stockmen who had ever ridden the ranges.

Even before he had pulled his horse's head round old Gene had leant over and grasped the bridle-rein with one hand, while with the other he wrapped the rider round in a grip of iron. As though at a prearranged signal, Pete and Monty dashed forward, and before he had time to barely gather what had happened, the lone horseman found himself held in a pair of brawny arms, which closed about his throat and prevented him from calling, while two more pairs of hands deftly bound and gagged him.

Then, after he had been strapped to the saddle, Monty took the bridle rein of the horse, and in this fashion Yvonne's little party moved back through the gate, their captive being helplessly led behind.

Old Gene closed the gate, and once more they spread out around the sheep, starting them on again across the Binabong paddocks to as strange a place of concealment as Nature in her most perverse mood ever provided.

Before Ike Vineburg and his crew had broken up the happiness of Yvonne's old home, and when she, in all her girlish lightheartedness, rode the paddocks which she loved, many and long were the journeys of exploration which she took into the great stretches of mysterious and fascinating scrub and gullies which lay in the very centre of the estate, and which were marked on the estate plan as "unknown rocky gullies and canyons— no grass, no water, no soil; inaccessible and barren; unexplored."

She made no mention of her lone journeys into the unknown heart of the estate, for the simple reason that such mention would have brought down her father's ban at once. Unsurveyed and unknown, this spot, which lay in the heart of Binabong like a stretch of wilderness in the midst of plenty, was the bugbear of every stockman and boundary rider in the district.

Once, when Binabong had great mobs of cattle roaming over it, there had been a stampede one night, and many hundred of cattle had disappeared over the mysterious edge of the wilderness—never to return. Mysterious, because the stockmen had followed their tracks to the edge of a cliff which seemed to drop into an eternity of rock and scrub, and which revealed no bottom.

After this it was given a wide berth, and went always by the appropriate, name of Death Valley.

About the same time a copy of the book which Campbell had read, and which Blake was reading that very evening, fell into Yvonne's hands. It didn't take her long to connect the mysterious spot on Binabong with the very place which Jackson, the bushranger, had used, the location of which had been forgotten after his death.

"If he and his companions know of a way into the seemingly

impenetrable fastness then, that way must still exist," argued Yvonne.

Forthwith she set out to explore still further, and how well her efforts succeeded will be seen as this story of her return to Binabong proceeds.

She and her companions paid little attention to the silent captive who was being led along in the rear. All their attention was given up to the sheep, for, as on previous nights, Yvonne wished to make the hiding-place by daybreak. Where it was a possibility to guide the sheep through the well-known paddocks by night, and to keep them in travelled stretches in order that their trail might be lost in the general maze of tracks of former mobs, it was another thing to get them into the hiding-place. For this daylight was essential, and yet it must not be too long after sun-up, for boundary riders have keen eyes, and they might be seen by one who happened to be crossing Binabong in order to cut off several miles of a journey.

On through paddock after paddock they went, Gene and the other stock-men working incessantly to keep the sheep on the move.

Finally, the friendly shadow of the big gum and box trees was left behind, and just as the first faint streak appeared in the east they broke out on stony ground.

Then did Yvonne take the lead.

In the cold dawn-light the country before them appeared to be a wilderness of scrubby, stony, rolling gullies and cliffs through which no man could possibly desire to pass.

Riding along a rocky valley between two breasting hills, Yvonne kept on to the far end, where the land suddenly dropped into a sheer cliff, whose base was hidden from view.

Opposite this another bulging cliff crossed at an angle, hiding from view the land beyond.

Yvonne paused on the very brink, and for a moment her eyes swept the barren, forbidding stretch of gullies. Then she turned her horse's head abruptly to the left, and disappeared over the brow of a hill into the midst of a stretch of open scrub. Behind her came the sheep being driven by the stockmen. At the bottom she turned along the bed of a dead watercourse, and for twenty minutes rode in silence. At the end of that time another sheer cliff appeared, and the tenderfoot would have sworn her horse was standing on the very spot it had stood on before.

It was not, however, but was only one of those baffling likenesses which befool men, and send them wandering for days until they know not where they are.

Once again Yvonne turned abruptly to the left, and for the second time rode through a patch of open scrub to the bottom of a gully. There she again followed the bed of a dead stream, this time for about ten minutes longer than before. These ten minutes were almost the sole proof that her course was a different one, and had an important bearing on the secret way, for it meant that all the time she was travelling in a vast circle, and the ever-increasing depths of the gullies indicated that she was ever getting lower.

Time after time she turned, until at last the bald edge of the gigantic cliff could be seen piercing the morning sky, their points and jagged corners stabbing the pink and gold like a multitude of minarets and domes. Lower and lower went Yvonne, her big roan picking his way with the surefootedness born of knowledge, for, indeed, he and the girl who swayed so easily to his every move had travelled that long descent many times.

At last she drew up and turned her head. Behind her came the dusty mob of sheep, with Gene and his companions, now the need for caution gone, shouting and hi-hi-ing the while they cracked and double-cracked their long stock-whips. Further in the rear rode the captive between Treherne and Graves, the latter puffing nonchalantly at his eternal cigarette.

With a sudden delicious laugh and a wave of her hand, Yvonne turned back, and spurred in through a short, shallow gully, until, on turning the bend, she came out suddenly upon as fair a view as Nature ever fashioned.

All around her, like a great wall, losing itself in the distance, stretched the giant cliffs, their sides sheer and impassable.

Before her was a vast expanse of riotous green dotted here and there by wide-spreading trees. From low down at one side a silver stream gushed out merrily, winding onwards through the dense green meadow like a white ribbon. Far away, near the centre, it trickled softly into a small lake, around the banks of which Yvonne knew Jameson's missing sheep would be clustered in lazy enjoyment of the early morning sun.

Although the extent of the place could not be seen from any one position, Yvonne knew, from many journeys around it, that it comprised some three thousand acres of rich grazing land always green and always watered. Immune from the most severe drought, hidden away from the outside world, guarded by a tortuous path which, until Yvonne had discovered it, had lain disused and unknown ever since Jackson, the bushranger, had died, it was truly a haven of solitude, an Arcadia for man or beast, an impregnable stronghold against an army.

Evidently the sheep thought so, at any rate, for as they entered the short gully which was the last stage of their journey, they scented the smell of the fresh green ahead. First the leaders lifted their heads and sniffed, then those behind got the scent. Forgetting their tired limbs and parched throats, the whole mob broke into a hopping run, and rushed pell-mell into the beautiful green stretch which unfolded itself before them.

Yvonne laughed softly at their silly antics as they gambolled away over the green, seeking the silver stream. Well she knew they needed no guard now. The trouble would be in persuading them to leave such an attractive spot. Gene and the others rode through the gully more slowly. Yvonne waited until they drew near, then signed to Graves to bring on the captive.

She gazed in puzzlement at the odd expression on her uncle's face as he rode forward, leading the captive's horse. She could not see the features of the prisoner himself, for the broad-brimmed soft felt hat he wore was pulled down over his eyes. As Graves drew close he raised one hand and swept the prisoner's hat from his head, and Yvonne found herself gazing into a pair of boyish eyes which she knew only too well.

"You!" she gasped in stupefaction.

"At your service, Mademoiselle Yvonne," came Tinker's voice, as he bowed stiffly.

For once in her life Yvonne was completely swamped for a reply. Evidently Graves was not above appreciating the situation, for he was smiling broadly at Yvonne's confusion.

"You! You!" she repeated feebly, as she sought to discover if she were dreaming.

"Again at your service," grinned the lad— "though I'd find it more comfortable if you would release my hands," he added.

"What are you doing here?" demanded Yvonne, regaining her self-possession.

"I really don't know," answered Tinker, "since I was brought here against my will."

"I don't mean that. What were you doing in Edward Jameson's paddock?"

"Trying to discover where his sheep were disappearing to, and I guess from the look of things I have found out."

Yvonne nodded her head thoughtfully.

"I suppose it is safe to assume that your master is also in Australia?" she said slowly.

Tinker smiled, but made no attempt to reply.

Yvonne turned and beckoned to Gene. When this old stock-man came up, she bent her head and whispered:

"Gene, yonder lad is the assistant of a man who has at times been an enemy and at times a friend. This time he happens to be on the side of the enemy, and for that reason that lad must not escape. He knows a thousand and one tricks for getting loose, so watch him carefully, Gene. When I tell you his master is the only man who can seriously menace our plans, you will understand how necessary it is that this lad be held."

"You leave it to me, missie," replied the stockman, dropping a caressing hand to the butt of his revolver. "If a youngster like that can best old Gene—well, then it is time I lost myself."

"All right, Gene; I leave him in your hands. Take him along to the bushrangers' huts, but keep him separated from our other prisoner."

She smiled mockingly at Tinker as Gene led him away, but the lad gave no sign.

Truth to tell, Tinker had been as dumbfounded at discovering Yvonne to be the cause of the mystery as she had been at seeing him in Australia. When he had ridden away from Campbell's station with the party which had been detailed to lend their assistance to Jameson, the present denouement had been most remote from his thoughts. He and Captain O'Brien had been amongst those who patrolled the boundary fence between Binabong and Walla-Walla.

For several hours they had kept together, sitting motionless in the shadow near the very mob of wethers which was to be Yvonne's objective that night. Then the impatient captain had ridden away in the hopes of running into the rustlers, leaving Tinker alone to guard the wethers.

The lad had shared the captain's opinion that, if the night were to see an attempt, it would be at another spot. He still stuck to his post, however, and the captain had been gone less than half an hour, when the soft click of the gate had warned him that someone was approaching.

Keyed up to the last pitch, he bent forward silently, the while he worked his revolver loose and held it ready. Then low voices broke on his ears, and his pulses raced as he realised that he and he alone was to be the only witness of another attempt.

For a moment he weighed the advisability of firing into the air in order to attract attention from others of the watchers who might be within hearing; but he realised that this would only alarm the rustlers, who would have every chance of getting away.

He resolved to sit tight and do nothing. Then, when they had departed with the sheep, he would creep after them, and track them to their destination. It was at that moment that a pure accident precipitated his advance, and caused all his careful plans to collapse into ignominious capture.

When the party of rustlers circled the mob, they passed very close to Tinker, and it was because he felt positive one of them had seen him that he boldly rode forward and attempted to bluff. He blamed himself afterwards for not firing to give the alarm, and ruining his chances of escaping, but it was one of those cases when all the forethoughts came as afterthoughts, and, really, circumstances were to blame, not the lad.

And now, here he was in possession of startling information which, unless he could escape, was useless. Even as old Gene led him away, however, his mind was busy with plans for escape. They had not blindfolded him on the way in, and Tinker felt that if he could once reach the gully, he could find his way out.

He and Graves had recognised each other when daylight had made their features distinguishable; but Yvonne's uncle, beyond a smile, had given no sign, and Tinker said nothing. All he wanted then, and all he wanted now, was to escape too close attention.

He had every cogent reason for wishing this, and it came from the fact that, all the way from the scene of his capture, he had been working surreptitiously at the cord which bound his wrists. The gag had been removed, but he knew he might as well shout for help in the middle of the Pacific Ocean as to expect to be heard from the depths of that fastness.

Evidently the stockman thought his bonds needed no examination, for he led the lad's horse along the base of the cliffs until he reached a tumbledown shanty which stood amongst others in a little grove of trees. There he lifted Tinker from the saddle, and carried him bodily into the hut. Tossing him into the corner with about as much ceremony as he would have bestowed upon a sack of flour, he calmly bit off a chew of tobacco and turned to leave.

At the door he paused.

"Now, young feller," he said, punctuating his words by tapping on the butt of his revolver "here you be, and here you stay! Understand?"

Tinker vouchsafed no reply.

"And if you try to escape—well, my son, I kin cut a rope with this little rib-tickler at some few paces, an' I warn you good and plenty that I ain't standin' no foolin'! Do you get me?"

"I get you, Steve," answered Tinker cheekily; and with an appreciative grin at the lad's spirit, old Gene withdrew.

But Tinker knew that, regardless of the smile, the stockman meant business, and would keep his word about shooting. Nevertheless, such knowledge did not deter him from his purpose, and he gave a grunt of satisfaction when he found his hands were not to be inspected.

"If I can get an hour without being interrupted," he muttered, "I can manage to get these things off, and then old grizzly will find two can play at the shooting game."

Barely had the rickety door closed behind Gene, when Tinker was once more at work. To saw at them was useless, for they were of tough cowhide, and the old hut contained nothing having a cutting edge which would go through that. Consequently, all he could do was to work patiently away, taking all the advantage he could from the careless knot.

As he felt the outer wrappings loosening he redoubled his energies. Slowly, by dint of twisting and turning his wrists, he managed to loosen the next layer then the next and the next, until finally he got one hand free, and the job was done. Exultant over his success, he was just about to creep over to the door to inspect the outside, when, without the slightest warning, it flew open to a heavy kick, and Gene thrust his grizzled head in.

Tinker drew his hands behind his back, and lay still, returning glance for glance as coolly as he could, though all the time his heart was beating madly as he wondered if the stockman suspected.

He breathed more easily when the door again closed.

"If he doesn't suspect now, the chances are he won't look in again for a little while," muttered the lad, "and if I am going to get away, I'd better make a move."

With infinite caution, he crept across to the rickety door which had lain so long in disuse. Owing to this, the action of the elements had provided it with numerous cracks, where the rotting boards had fallen apart. Through one of these Tinker peeped, and seeing no signs of movement outside, stealthily pushed open the door a few inches, and thrust out his head.

Everything was as still as the grave. The sun, now high in the heavens, beat down warmly on the little Arcadia, and the green glade in which the huts were nestled seemed already drowsy with the warmth. A few birds twittered in the trees overhead, but of human beings there were no signs.

After a moment's inspection Tinker opened the door still wider and slipped through. He paused only long enough to close it; then, taking cover in the trees, he sped softly through the glade until he came to an open patch. Beyond, in a bed of green, he could see the little stream, while still further along he could make out the figures of three horsemen. He did not know it then, but Yvonne, with Treherne, Graves, and three of the stockmen had already started for Binabong homestead, leaving Gene and three of his companions to guard the prisoners and the sheep.

Even as the lad surveyed the three horsemen who were on their way to the lake, was Gene in another hut attending to the other prisoner.

Tinker, seeing the coast comparatively clear, wasted no time, and risked a dash across the open space until he reached the cover of another clump of trees. In this way he made his way in alternate dashes and reconnoitrings until he had left the huts a good half-mile behind. Then the mouth of the gully came into view, and he risked all on one mad rush.

He had hoped to be able to find the horses on his way, but saw no signs of them, and dared not risk a delay. He reached the mouth of the gully panting, and paused to look back.

At that moment the sound of a shot from a heavy calibred

revolver floated across the still air. He saw the three distant horsemen wheel and gaze back. It didn't need much to make him realise that the shot had come from Gene's gun, and, turning sharply, he sped swiftly along the gully.

Again a shot rang out, then three others more distant sounded in answer.

The horsemen had heard the alarm. Tinker's escape had been discovered. In five minutes they would be in pursuit.

And Tinker, running with a regular lope, fought down his inclination to increase his pace, for he realised it was a long stiff trail out of that spot, and he would need every ounce of strength he possessed if he were to reach the top before his mounted pursuers.

Harris swung round like lightning, dropping his hand to his hip. "I shou.dn't do that if I were you," drawled Blake.
(See page 16.)

Sexton Blake's dramatic meeting with Yvonne on the Binabong Estates.

THE FOURTH CHAPTER.   Blake Gets on Tinker's Track— And Meets Yvonne.

Though Sexton Blake spent far into the night poring over the old book which dealt with the doings of Jackson, the bushranger, there were still no signs of the returning party when he put out his light and retired.

His host had gone to his room early, in order to be in good trim for the morrow.

Even when Blake rose the next morning Captain O'Brien, Tinker, and the younger Campbell had not returned. He joined Captain Campbell, and together they made a run for the big cement swimming-tank, which was fed from the artesian bore.

They were still splashing about in the cold, bracing water when the captain and the younger Campbell entered, looking tired from their night in the saddle, and covered from head to foot in the dust of the paddocks.

"Well, did you catch the rustlers?" called Blake from where he stood poised on the springboard ready to dive.

The usually cheerful captain looked strangely serious.

"No," he replied, shaking his head; "but they got away with a mob of sheep just the same."

"You fellows deserve a medal," jeered Campbell. "It's a wonder they didn't get away with one of you as well."

"They did," answered the captain shortly.

"Who?" demanded Campbell incredulously.

"Where is Tinker?" broke in Blake suddenly.

The captain lifted his hands helplessly.

"That is what we have been trying to find out ever since two o'clock last night."

"Do you mean to say they got him?" asked Blake sharply, as he reached for a towel.

The captain nodded.

"Yes, and in a way I blame myself for it. But get dressed, you chaps, and I'll tell you everything when we get to the house."

Blake was already getting into his bath-robe, and Campbell lost no time in following suit. Then the quartet made their way to the house, where Blake signed to the captain to proceed with his story.

"I'm awfully sorry, old man," he said soberly. "I know how you must feel, and I'll be as brief as possible."

Blake made a gesture, and the captain continued.

"When we reached Walla-Walla, we placed ourselves at Jameson's disposal. He divided us into pairs, and spread us clear round the boundary fences. Tinker and I happened to get paired, and went on guard in one of the far paddocks which adjoins Binabong. We had a distance of four miles to patrol, and on my advice we took up our position in about the middle of our beat.

"My idea was to put in some time there; then I would ride two miles in one direction, and on my return Tinker would ride the other two miles. The only sheep near our beat were mobbed up for the night right near the middle, and this influenced my plan, for you can see one of us would have them under observation continually.

"Well, I suppose I was beginning to get impatient. At any rate, as we hadn't heard a sound I thought I would do my two miles, and ride along the next beat to see if the other party had heard anything. This I did, leaving Tinker to watch the sheep. I was gone about three hours altogether, and when I returned gave the whistle on which we had arranged.

"I got no reply, and, on riding nearer to where Tinker had been left, I saw that not a single sheep was on the spot where the mob had been when I departed. I whistled again, and still heard nothing.

"Then, feeling that something must be wrong, I rode as fast as I could back the way I had just come, until I picked up two of the Walla-Walla stockmen who were on the next beat. I told them what had happened, and one of them came back with me while the other went to spread the alarm.

"In half an hour we had about thirty men on the scene with lights.

"For the first time since the Jameson's sheep have been disappearing there seemed a definite clue. Right near where the wethers were there is a big cyclone gate set in. By their lights the stockmen followed the tracks of the sheep through this gate and into the adjoining Binabong paddock. At the very most, supposing the sheep had been driven off immediately after my departure, they couldn't be very far away.

"We spread out in a great circle, and rode straight across Binabong in a way which we felt must pick up the sheep. Daylight came then, and helped us considerably; but, will you believe it, those sheep might have vanished into the air for all the sign we saw of them?"

"How about the tracks from the gate?" asked Campbell quickly.

"The stockmen went back there, but it did no good. We followed them to the gate all right, and can swear they passed through, but there the trail ends. The whole place is covered with a maze of sheep-tracks made during several months. In places the top layer of ground has pulverised and broken into dust, but generally the place still retains the tracks. There seemed to be a general tendency of the freshly trampled ground to run in one direction. This we followed, and finally decided that it must be the trail of the sheep. It ended abruptly on stony ground, however, and from that we lost it.

"They are still searching, and may run up against something at any moment. We have hunted high and low for Tinker, but he seems to have vanished as utterly as have the sheep. We thought the best thing to do was to ride on here at once and tell you, for we know Blake would wish to know."

When the captain had finished Blake looked thoughtful.

Campbell appeared to be turning over in his mind the question of the trail.

Finally Blake spoke. "You say that what you took for tracks ended in stony ground?" he said slowly.

The captain nodded.

"Yes."

"Is this ground you speak of very extensive?"

"Yes, it stretches away until it develops into a big expanse of country, which lies in the middle of Binabong. It is called Death Valley, and certainly looks the part. It is nothing but a wilderness of stone and scrub, breaking into gullies and cliffs, quite impassable, and absolutely barren."

"I see," responded Blake. Then, turning to his host, he said, "Have you a surveyor's map of the district?"

"Oh, yes! There is one in my office which was made out about ten years ago. Of course, this district has never been surveyed in detail, but it gives a fair idea of the country and the boundaries are pretty correct."

"I will go along to the office with you and have a look at it," answered Blake.

"What do you want us to do?" asked the captain. "Shall we go back and join in the search for Tinker, or would you rather we waited for you?"

Blake stood in thought for a few moments.

"There seems no doubt but that the lad has gone the way of the sheep," he said slowly; "but, in my opinion, neither they nor he will be rescued by force. The only thing which will meet the case will be strategy. Numbers will spoil that, so I would suggest you get some rest. I have no definite theory yet, but I may have after I have seen the plan. In any case, I shall start out soon to search for him, and will work alone. On the whole, I think you had better retire."

"Gad! I can't do that!" exclaimed the captain. "I feel half responsible for his disappearance, so if I can't be of any assistance to you I will return and help the others."

"All right," said Blake, "Suit yourself."

The younger Campbell evidently felt as the captain did, for he accompanied the latter outside, and shortly after the clatter of the horses' hoofs could be heard as they galloped away.

Campbell wore a puzzled look as he led the way to his office. He had read much of the doings of his old school friend, and, in common with everyone else felt that Blake was well-nigh infallible.

On the present occasion, however, he considered that the subject in hand was more in the line of the stockmen than in that of the brilliant detective, even though the latter had spent a good part of his time with stock. He failed utterly to understand why Blake wanted to see the surveyor's map, but as host it was not up to him to question his guest's strange fancy.

The map itself was a faded blue print, which certainly looked its age. When Campbell had unfolded it and handed it to him Blake spread it out on the desk and studied it closely.

For half an hour he gave no sign; then he turned, and said briefly:

"I hear the sound of horse's hoofs, Dumpy; would you mind seeing who it is? I think you will find it is someone bringing word that Tinker's horse has returned riderless."

Campbell glanced at him in surprise, but said nothing as he hurried out.

Less than a minute later he was back, looking more surprised than ever.

"Well, I'm dashed if I can see how you knew it," he blurted out, "but you are right."

"Exactly," smiled Blake. "Horse returned in fresh condition —

not hungry, nor thirsty. Am I right?"

Campbell nodded.

"Yes. By heavens! Right in every particular!"

"That is what I was waiting for," said Blake, rising. "And now, if you will order a horse for me I shall start out."

"Hadn't I better come along with you?"

Blake shook his head the while he slipped a fresh clip in his automatic.

"No, I'd rather go alone, if you don't mind. I shall take Pedro along with me. To tell you the truth, I have a certain theory. If I am right, it will need great caution. On the other hand, I may be wrong, so I shall go off on my own and investigate. In the meantime, the others can be keeping up their search."

"All right," laughed Campbell ruefully. "I'm hanged if I follow your line of reasoning, but you seem to have a clue which I haven't."

"My dear chap, you yourself gave me the only clue I have." smiled Blake.

"I!" echoed the other.

"Yes. If it turns out to be worth anything I shall tell you all about it later."

With that Campbell had to be content. Five minutes later Blake was in the saddle. He had fashioned a long leash for Pedro, who was to accompany him. Hanging from the saddle was a water-bottle, and in his pocket a large packet of sandwiches. Evidently Blake expected his search to consume a fair amount of time.

Waving his hand to his host he took a hitch in Pedro's leash. Then he dug his heels in his horse, and went galloping away in the direction of Walla-Walla.

Though the lay mind might have made some connection between the story of Jackson, the bushranger and Jameson's remarkable tale, it would also dismiss the connection as coincidence.

To begin with, the bushranger had lived half a century before, and in that time the tales of many of his doings had been so exaggerated by constant repetition that, in a way, it was difficult to say what was fact and what was fiction.

On the head of this, hundreds of experienced stockmen had at different times searched for the mysterious place where he was supposed to have concealed the cattle he had stolen; and the very fact that no such place had ever been discovered seemed to stamp that story as being pure romance.

Death Valley had, amongst other places, been considered, but the oldest man in the district would tell you that it was nothing but an impassable stretch of rocky scrub and cliffs which no man had ever crossed, and no man would, and if any man tried he would be a fool.

Consequently, it had never entered the heads of the searchers after Jameson's sheep that Death Valley might, after all, contain grass in the midst of its rocky ravines, and, even if it had, they would have scouted the idea as preposterous. At first blush Blake had been inclined to share this opinion, but while the others had been excitedly discussing the affair, his mind had seized upon one item and around it he had built.

That item was the disappearance of one of Jameson's stockmen, and the subsequent return of his horse in a fresh condition.

"In the first place," he mused, "all highly coloured theories must be abandoned. Here we have the regular disappearance of good-sized mobs of sheep. Jameson and his men have scoured the district in the most thorough manner. That means, no matter how impossible it may seem, they are not far away. Secondly, the disappearance of his stockman and the return of his horse lends colour to this theory.

"Then, is there any stretch of land in this district which is untravelled, and which is extensive enough to provide feed for such a number of sheep? If so, why hasn't it been searched?

"Item two: What is the possibility of any connection between the old bushranger tale and this mystery?

"Item three: The very mystery of the affair proclaims the possibility of a simple solution.

"Query: Why is Jameson the sole victim, and what motive can there be?

"On Jameson's own showing he is at loggerheads with his neighbour Treherne, and even goes so far as to say he suspects the latter. Why? If their relations are as Jameson says, Treherne would not be fool enough to do anything so serious for the sake of petty revenge.

"Item: Look up story in the book which deals with the bushranger and examine a survey map of the district.''

Thus far had Blake's mind worked on the night before. Following up these suggestions, he had, as will be remembered, spent some time reading the book. Then he had searched the survey map. One place, and one place only, was marked on the old blue print as being unknown. It was Death Valley, and on the map was classified "Unknown barren stretch. Rocky and scrubby gullies and cliffs. No feed. No water. Dangerous for stock. Unexplored."

Before the captain and the younger Campbell returned, Blake had formed a tentative theory based on those arguments. True, the disappearance of Jameson's stockman may have been an isolated event; but if the same thing happened again—well, it would strengthen his theory that both sheep and men were near at hand. It had happened again, and its effect had come closer to Blake than to anyone else, for Tinker had been the second victim.

Something of the same line of thought was in his mind as he cantered through the paddocks and turned through the gate lending to Walla-Walla. He did not stop at the homestead to see Jameson, but kept on to the scene of the disappearance.

There he found everything just as the captain had said.

The ground, hard though it was, presented a scuffled appearance where the wethers had been, it was easy enough to follow their tracks through the gateway, and from where he stood Blake thought he could make out the darker coloured line which, in the opinion of the stockmen, marked the course taken by the sheep.

Instead of following this up until he came to the spot where the tracks were lost on strong ground, Blake slipped out of the saddle, and tied his horse to the fence.

"There is one thing certain," he muttered thoughtfully, as he surveyed the ground. "In driving off those sheep during the night they had to be mighty quiet, and, unless I am mistaken, it was done by stock-whips, and on foot. Anyway, that is a bare chance."

He tied Pedro's leash to the fence, and, drawing out his powerful pocket glass, he dropped to his knees in the midst of the tracks and went to work. Jameson's stockmen had already been over the spot both on foot and mounted, and Blake realised he had his work cut out to find that for which he sought. He knew it would be a mere waste of time to search in the main body of the tracks, for there, if anywhere, would he get confused.

Consequently, he knelt close to the boundary fence where his only chance of success lay. Lying flat, he held the glass close to the ground, and in this fashion crept slowly along, stopping at intervals, until he reached the cyclone gate. Each time he had stopped he had uttered a grunt of satisfaction, but, beyond this, it was impossible to tell how he was making out. Opening the gate, he again dropped to the ground, and in this manner crept through into the adjoining Binabong paddock.

It seemed an utter impossibility for any man to find anything distinctive in the trampled ground which met Blake there. What with the passage of thousands of sheep during the dry months and the tracks left by Jameson's stockmen, the place left little for even Blake's keen eyes to seize upon. He persevered, however, and after twenty minutes' solid work, he rose, dusty, but triumphant.

He had found little, it is true. Only the partial impression of a heavy heel with three little boles along the edge, showing where the nails had protruded a trifle. But, this same impression was that which he had followed on the other side of the fence, and, from its very proximity to the boundary, he knew it was a good gamble that it belonged to one of the rustlers.

Stepping back through the gateway, he untied Pedro, and led him along to the first impression he had examined. There he gave the bloodhound sufficient time to get the scent well before he mounted. It was only a chance, and Blake knew it, but if Pedro couldn't trace the rustlers after their visible tracks had become obliterated on the stony ground, then nobody could. The scent he intended following might turn out to be one of Jameson's stockmen, and then it would be only so much time wasted. That was a chance which must be risked.

Pedro was already straining at the leash, and, stopping only long enough to close the gate, Blake started his horse. Away they went across the Binabong paddocks, Pedro travelling strongly and Blake keeping pace. As yet he had seen no signs of any of the other searchers. He judged, and rightly, that they had again drawn a blank.

In one thing he saw the stockmen had been correct. The slightly discoloured streak of soil was undoubtedly the trail of the sheep, for Pedro stuck to it closely. Until he reached the stony ground, however, Blake could not tell for certain whether he had struck the trail of one of the rustlers or that of some stockman.

He was not to be kept in ignorance long, for, as he breasted a low ridge, he saw the slope ahead dip away, the grass suddenly grow sparse, and, further on, a wide expanse of stony ground which stretched away like a chill, grey sea to break in rocky waves against a veritable wilderness in the distance.

"So that is where Death Valley lies," he muttered, pulling up. "It certainly doesn't look as though it could possibly conceal anything attractive, and I don't wonder the stockmen give it a wide berth."

He started again, and, on reaching the stony ground, smiled grimly, for Pedro kept straight on in the direction of the wilderness.

All visible tracks had disappeared. Only the rough, barren stone remained, but that seemed to matter little to the bloodhound. On he went, drawing nearer and nearer to the uninviting desolation ahead. Suddenly he swung to the right and skirted the edge of a sickly-looking bunch of scrub. For twenty minutes he travelled thus, until the stony ridges broke into a deep gully, and down this Pedro turned.

Barely had he started along it, however, when he suddenly stopped and began worrying about. Around and around he went, seeking for the scent which he had lost. Blake dismounted, and led him about in ever-growing circles, but all Pedro's efforts were useless.

"Ah!" grunted Blake. "That should have occurred to me. The rustler probably mounted his horse here. Never mind, old chap," he added aloud. "You have shown the way, at least, and we'll follow it as well as we can."

He was just on the point of remounting when the sound of pounding hoofs broke on his ears. Springing into the saddle, he swung his horse, and, pulling on the leash, dashed into a patch of dense scrub just as four horsemen swept up the gully and pulled up not ten yards from where he was concealed.

Blake drew his revolver and leaned forward. He could see their faces plainly, and as they began to speak he listened.

"He never got this far, Gene," one of them was saying, "He must have heard us coming, and probably took into the scrub along one of the gullies."

"I'm thinking he never came up the trail at all," broke in another. "In my opinion he is still back in the bottom lying low and waiting his chance."

Blake was shrewd enough to guess that they were discussing the escape of someone, and he devoutly hoped it was Tinker. Had he known, however, of the awful experience the lad was to have, he would have devoutly wished the opposite. As the man called Gene began to speak, Blake bent forward still more in order to catch what he said.

"Either of you may be right," he said savagely. "Anyway, he was game, and we must catch him. You stay up here, Harris, and watch for him. We will ride back to the bottom and search there. He won't keep his freedom long."

Harris nodded, and dropped his bridle rein over his horse's neck the while he began to roll a cigarette. Without further words, Gene and the other two turned and clattered back down the gully. Harris's back was towards the man who was concealed in the scrub, and, as he lazily puffed at his cigarette, he did not see the steady hand which lifted a business-like looking automatic.

He heard the swish of the bushes, and the ring of the horse's hoofs as Blake rode out, however, and swung like lightning, dropping his hand to his hip.

"I wouldn't do that if I were you," drawled Blake. "Put your hands up. Quick!"

Harris wavered; then, quelled by the look in the other's eye, obeyed.

"That's better," said Blake. "Just keep them up and let me suggest that you try no games. This trigger is balanced very delicately, and a sudden movement on your part, might cause trouble."

"Who the devil are you, and what do you want?" growled Harris.

"Who I am doesn't concern you," answered Blake. "As to what I want, you will find out in good time. First, I want that revolver of yours."

He rode forward as he spoke, until the shoulder of his horse was against, that of Harris's horse. Then, still keeping his man covered, Blake bent quickly, and jerked the other's gun from its holster.

"Now we can talk more comfortably," he said backing his horse away. "Lower your hands."

Harris obeyed.

"Put them behind you."

Again the command was obeyed.

"Keep them there, and Heaven help you if you try any funny business."

"It seems to me you are pretty high-handed, mister," grunted Harris.

"Do you think so?" remarked Blake pleasantly, again riding forward. "Now then cross your wrists. That's it, my friend. Steady now, and we'll have you trussed up beautifully."

As he spoke, Blake was working busily at the other's hands. Using a strap from his saddle bags he tied them deftly, and when he had finished, lifted the bridle rein of Harris's horse, and threw it around his prisoner's neck.

"That will help to keep your horse from stumbling." he remarked in the same deadly pleasant voice which was beginning to make his prisoner glance at him with new respect. "Now then," went on Blake, "just prod your animal gently, my friend, and lead the way into this place."

Harris eyed Blake truculently, then he glanced at Pedro. "I don't know who in blazes you are," he grumbled, "but if you want to go in here, come on."

With that he prodded his horse, and led the way. Blake followed, leading Pedro, and in this fashion the little procession started.

Blake knew very well that he was, so to speak, entering the jaws of the tiger. Up to now he had no idea of the organising brain behind the sheep stealing, and what he had seen so far, convinced him that it must be an ordinary case of stock rustling. Still he held his final judgment in abeyance, realising that while he was risking all on entering Death Valley, he had a gambling chance in that he possessed a hostage.

He had been in positions of a similar nature to that of his prisoner's, and he knew full well what was going on in the latter's mind. His ready acquiescence had not fooled Blake. At the top of the gully, bound and helpless, Harris had no chance, while at the bottom of the wilderness there were friends who would use their best endeavours to free him.

Besides, he must feel that he had been negligent in the pursuit of his duty, so easily had he been captured. Altogether, he stood more chance by obeying Blake's orders than in disobeying them, so having made his decision, he urged his horse to the descent.

As they travelled along the tortuous path, which Yvonne had discovered, Blake kept his eyes open, taking in all the peculiarities and landmarks of the trail. Slowly, as they went along, he was taking a mental photograph of the way which would never fade; and, did circumstances arise which made it necessary for him to make a sudden retreat, he would know his way. Turning after turning they took until Harris reached the short gully which led into Yvonne's retreat.

Blake had no idea how far down the bottom might be, but he was sharp enough to know that it could not be much farther. Unless the height of the surrounding cliffs were of no indication, then the steady descent must be bringing them near their goal. He marvelled at the intricate trail, which in itself formed such an impregnable bulwark, and he looked forward with no little interest to seeing what might lie hidden in the heart of this rocky, forbidding wilderness.

He began closing up gradually on his prisoner, and when they turned the last bend, Blake was close behind. Then the whole beauty of the retreat lay spread before them.

Blake gave an involuntary gasp of pleasure as he saw it, but quickly turned his attention back to his prisoner, who had a suspicious look in his eye.

"Ah! would you?" snapped Blake, spurring forward and clapping his hand over Harris's mouth just as the latter opened it to give a yell of warning to his friends. "I guess you will do better with a gag between your teeth, my friend. I'll supply that deficiency, and then you can rusticate in the scrub whilst I investigate this Arcadia."

Suiting the action to the word, Blake gagged his prisoner and tied a handkerchief over his mouth. Then he slipped out of the saddle, and dragged Harris to the ground. Half carrying, half dragging him, he made his way into the scrub which lined the sides of the gully, and secured his prisoner to a tree. This done, he led the horses in, and tied them also. Releasing Pedro's leash, he pointed to the prisoner.

"Watch him!" he ordered, and even as Blake crept away down the gully, Pedro was sitting in front of Harris making that veteran decidedly uncomfortable by the exhibition of a set of wicked-looking teeth.

On reaching the grassy bottom, Blake reconnoitred. At first he could make out no signs of the men whom he sought. What he did see, however, was the group of huts, and towards these he began to creep. Using practically the same methods which Tinker had used in leaving the place he wormed his way along, taking advantage of every bit of cover which offered, and dashing quickly across the open spaces. He reached the first hut without being seen, and lay in the grass behind it watching for signs of life.

Barely had he gained that position, when a door in one of the other huts slammed, and old Gene came along. He was heading for the hut behind which Blake lay concealed, and the detective could see he wore a decidedly savage expression. Whether or no his companions were about Blake had no idea. If they were they were keeping mighty quiet.

As though in answer to his thought there suddenly appeared, far in the distance, two horsemen. Then Blake remembered what had been said at the top of the gully about searching the bottom for the escaping prisoner.

By this time, Gene had drawn close, and gripping his revolver Blake made a quick decision. Rising like a shadow he levelled his aim and said:

"I'll trouble you to put your hands up."

The old stockman stopped dead in his tracks, and gazed in stupefaction at the apparition which had risen from the grass.

"What the—" he began.

"Up with them, my friend," drawled Blake. "Don't hitch that way. That's better. Now turn round and stand still." Striding forward, he jerked Gene's revolver from the holster as he had that of Harris. He was casting about for something with which to tie his prisoner when he was startled by a loud voice which came from the hut.

"I say, who is out there?"

"Who are you?" called back Blake, seeing Gene made no sign.

"A prisoner. Are you a friend?"

"Yes. Are you bound?"

"My hands are."

"Can you kick open the door, and come out?"

"I think I can manage it."

Silence reigned for a few moments. Then came a pounding noise as the man in the hut kicked at the rickety door. A moment later it flew out, and the dishevelled figure of a stockman stumbled out.

He gazed in open-mouthed astonishment at the sight which met him.

"I heard you hold up, Gene," he said, "and hoped it was a friend."

Blake nodded.

"Come along here, and I will cut your bonds."

The man obeyed. Blake kept Gene covered with the revolver while he drew out his knife and severed the cords which bound the other.

"Now then, take off your belt and tie up our friend," he said when he had finished. "I imagine it will be a pleasant duty."

"You just bet it will." answered the other grimly.

"Well hurry up," rapped Blake. "There are two more in the distance, and they are coming this way."

The released man needed no further bidding, and, though Gene looked as though he would like to fight, the steadily held automatic was a powerful argument, and he submitted. A minute later, with a gag between his teeth, he was occupying the hut in place of his late prisoner.

The two horsemen were riding along the bank of the stream drawing closer every moment. Blake surveyed them from the shelter of a clump of trees, then he turned to the man, he had released.

"I suppose you are the stockman from Walla-Walla who was caught." he said.

"Yes." nodded the other.

"What is your name?" asked Blake.

"Richards."

"Well, Richards, we have got to get that pair. I think the best plan is to take cover, and fire a shot. They will take that as a signal from their companion, and will ride up. As they approach we can keep them covered. It ought not to be very difficult for you to remove their weapons and tie them while I show them the business end of my automatic."

"I guess you are right." answered Richards. "You sure took old Gene neat."

"I have another up the gully," said Blake. "Now then, to cover, Richards."

They sank down behind a clump of bushes close to the path, which led between the huts. When they were settled, Blake lifted his revolver and fired a single shot.

A few minutes later, they heard the hurried clatter of hoofs drawing near, and the two horsemen came riding at a canter along the path.

"Now," whispered Blake.

With one accord they leaped out, and covered their men. The two horsemen jerked their horses back on their haunches, and their hands flew to their hips. The steely eyes and set jaw behind that black automatic convinced them that Blake meant business, and in obedience to his sharp command, their hands went up.

"Now then, Richards, look alive," jerked Blake. "Toss out their guns and tie their hands behind them."

Nothing loth, the stockman leaped to do Blake's bidding. Remembering his own recent plight he was far from gentle in his methods, and, by the time the new arrivals fully realised what was happening, they were securely bound.

"Fetch out Gene, and mount him." commanded Blake.

Richards did so, and at Blake's further command ran up a horse for himself.

"Now, my friends," went on Blake addressing his prisoners. "We are going out of here. My companion will lead the way. You will follow, and I will bring up the rear. We make one stop in order to pick up your other companion. Beyond that, I wouldn't advise you to attempt to stop or to play any hanky-panky tricks. Now then, march!"

And they marched, or at least their horses marched.

Blake walked behind until they reached the mouth of the gully where he had left Harris and Pedro. There he got his own horse, and assisting Harris into the saddle, the procession again started. They had covered perhaps half the distance when the sound of flying hoofs reached their ears, and Blake gripped his revolver as he saw the look of hope which overspread the faces of his prisoners.

Nearer and nearer came the sound until, on rounding a bend, they caught sight of a mounted figure riding recklessly down the trail. The rider was a woman, and Blake gazed in utter bewilderment as he recognised the features of Mademoiselle Yvonne.

Pedro, sitting in front of Harris, made that worthy uncomfortable by the exhibition of a wicked-looking set of teeth. (*See page 16.*)

The dishevelled stockman in the broken doorway gazed with amazement at the scene before him. (*See page 16.*)

THE FIFTH CHAPTER. Yvonne v. Jameson— His Threat— The Attack.

While Blake had been following up his theories, startling events had been taking place elsewhere—events which culminated in Yvonne's unexpected appearance at Death Valley.

To say that Edward Jameson was dumbfounded at still another disappearance of sheep was to put it mildly. Nor were his feelings salved by the additional information that one of Campbell's guests had also been spirited away. Practical to the last degree, it was difficult for one of his temperament to see aught in the series of outrages but the bold operations of an exceptionally clever band of stock rustlers. And yet the very lack of that sensitive fineness which was such an inherent part of Sexton Blake was the very thing which finally caused Jameson to experience the same indefinable feeling of rage which had already gripped the men on his place.

Put any one of them on a bucking horse, and he would stick to it until the beast was conquered; send him into a mob of cattle to cut out a steer, and he would sweep into that ocean of horns without a second's hesitation. Those things a stockman could feel and could understand. They were living and tangible. But this uncanny spiriting away of whole mobs of sheep was unnerving, to say the least, and the bush-bred stockmen made no bones about saying so.

For all his vast acres, Jameson was of the same stock as they, and when he did begin to waver he went down with a crash. What it was, who it was, how it was, he could not fathom, but in the yielding of his practical judgment he yielded also that veneer which went with his acres.

Like a mad bull who sees red, he became consumed with a terrific infuriation, a wild impulse to grip something tangible and blindly crush it between his great hands. And as Fate would have it, his thoughts turned in that moment of rage to the man whom he felt was responsible in some mysterious manner for his troubles—John Treherne.

Hot on the thought, with his rage still seething, he ordered a horse and, while his men were scouring the countryside in search of the missing sheep, Jameson himself was on his way to Binabong, intent on vengeance. He arrived there shortly after the return of Yvonne and her companions from seeing the sheep safely into Death Valley.

They were by no means surprised at seeing him approach, for by Yvonne's reckoning he should have taken the bait ere this. It had been her purpose to mystify and puzzle him, in order that he might make some move whereby she could confront him with the facts. If she could lure him into doing something rash, so much the better.

As they saw him sweeping up through the home paddock, Yvonne smiled a brief smile.

"Our neighbour, Mr. Jameson, of Walla-Walla, is coming," she said. "If I am any judge of facial expression, I would say that he is in a towering rage, and its cause, I imagine, comes from the fact that he feels the disappearance of his sheep emanates from Binabong, and yet he doesn't know."

Graves smiled, and lit a cigarette. He looked forward with keen relish to the coming visit. As for Treherne, he was nervously gnawing at his under lip. Although he had witnessed visible proof of Yvonne's brilliant generalship, and though the whole-hearted worship of Gene and his companions impressed him considerably, he had yet to see her wriggle herself free from the undoubted gravity of the situation.

The fact that her bridge to success was to be his "assignment of honour" of Binabong to Edward Jameson, did not tend to lessen the unpleasant prospect which he saw ahead. However, he had bound himself to do as Yvonne said, and now that the crisis had arrived there was nothing to do but meet it.

Jameson wasted little ceremony at the door. Throwing his bridle rein over a post, he stamped heavily up on the verandah and pounded at the wire door. Without waiting for his summons to be answered, he threw it open and marched down the hall. At the door of the room where he had gambled so successfully against Treherne he paused, and his teeth bared in a half snarl as he saw the three figures within.

"Treherne," he snapped, "I have business with you—private business. You may not wish to have me speak of it before your guests."

"My guests will remain, Jameson," answered Treherne quietly. "Whatever you have to say, say it before them."

"I will do so," replied the other, tossing his hat on the table. "In the first place, I presume you will not deny that I practically saved you from ruin during this drought?"

Treherne made a gesture, but did not speak.

"And I doubt if you will deny that I loaned you money, on your stock. Do you?"

"I do not."

"Nor will you deny that after that I loaned you a further sum on the property itself?"

"I do not."

"Very well. In my pocket I hold your written assignment of the place. You have seen fit to ignore that. You offered to take up the loans as though this assignment did not exist. We have had some strange types of Englishmen out here, John Treherne, but of all the types I think you are the worst. It has always been an Englishman's boast that he paid his debts of honour."

The blood rushed into Treherne's checks, then receded and left them white as paper as he heard Jameson's taunt. His hands clenched convulsively, and he half started up. A warning gesture from Yvonne, however, recalled him, and he sat silent.

"So that fails to move you, does it?" sneered Jameson. "A coward as well as a defaulter, eh! Well, look here, Treherne. This is my final word. I give you two hours to vacate Binabong. At the end of that time I shall treat you as a common trespasser and evict you. I have the law on my side and, if necessary, I shall use force."

"When you speak of eviction, you are addressing the wrong person, Mr. Jameson," broke in a cool, silvery voice.

Jameson swung and contemptuously regarded the slim girl who had spoken.

"Might I ask in what way?" he demanded sarcastically.

"Certainly," answered Yvonne. "Mr. Treherne does not happen to be the owner of Binabong."

"Indeed! I am afraid I do not understand you."

"No? Then I will enlighten you. Binabong was sold and legally transferred by Mr. Treherne yesterday, the purchaser assuming all his liabilities, Mr. Jameson."

"So he is a swindler as well!" snapped Jameson.

"In what way?"

"By selling that which did not belong to him."

"That is a point on which I do not agree with you."

"You seem to be pretty well informed, madam. Perhaps you will tell me next that you are the purchaser."

"Marvellous!" returned Yvonne. "How did you guess it?"

"I don't know what your game is," blazed Jameson, losing his head under her cool mockery, "but I can tell you this. Whichever of you owns this place you have my orders to vacate. At the end of two hours I will return with my men, and if you are not gone I shall deal with you in my own way."

"You will make that move by the authority of the assignment you hold from Mr. Treherne, I suppose?" drawled Graves.

"Certainly."

"Then 1 would suggest that several minutes of the two hours have already elapsed," broke in Yvonne. "Good-morning, Mr. Jameson."

For a moment Jameson glared at her. Then, turning on his heel, he picked up his hat. At the door he paused.

"I suppose you think I don't suspect who got away with my sheep," he jerked. "Well, I do. I don't know how you did it, but, by heaven, let me tell you I mean business! Remember, two hours!"

With that he stamped out and threw himself into the saddle. As he galloped away from the house, Yvonne rose and stood before Treherne.

"Cheer up, Mr. Treherne," she said, smiling. "You did nobly to restrain yourself under his insults. But, never mind, you will have a chance yet to get your own back."

"I am in your hands," answered Treherne. "It was mighty hard to be called a defaulter over a debt of honour, though!"

"I know, but it couldn't be helped. We want Edward Jameson to make exactly the move he threatened to make, and had we shown our hand everything would have fizzled out. But he means business, all right. He had vengeance in his eye, and hasn't the faintest idea that we know the truth about the playing cards. He judges others from his own point of view, which is clumsy. Had the same thing happened to him, he would have exposed the perpetrator at once. Mr. Jameson is not the type of man who appreciates or understands subtlety in others, though in his own crude way he has a vague notion of that quality, as witness his manipulation of the marked cards.

"However, there is no time to be lost. We are prepared for a siege, and Jameson will make one. Our prisoners form a complication, for we are short handed. Gene and the other three stockmen must be brought back here. I myself will ride to Death Valley and bring them. You, uncle, see about the guns and ammunition. Mr. Treherne can ride to the bunk-house for the men who are there. Then lock up.

"I do not know that I can make the valley and return in the two hours. At any rate, if Jameson attacks before I return, don't wait for us. Barricade the doors and windows and hold the place. I have always the winning card, so if the worst comes to the worst I can play that. The main point is to have Jameson attack us. I am sorry that it means risking life, but it is the only way, now we have gone so far."

"Do you think Blake is really here?" asked Graves.

"I don't know," answered Yvonne. "It seems as though he must be, and yet if that is so, and he is working with Jameson, it is strange that we have seen nothing of him. Perhaps Tinker is out here alone. I will endeavour to find out at Death Valley. And now I must be gone. Don't forget. If Jameson shows up before I return, don't wait. Let him fire the first shot; if he goes far, then retaliate, but not until you have to."

"I wish you would let me ride to the valley," said Treherne. "You may run into them on your way back, and in Jameson's present mood he will not be inclined to treat you gently."

"I can take care of myself." laughed Yvonne.

She turned as she spoke and slipped a small automatic into the holster at her belt. Picking up her gauntlets, she waved her hand and hurried out. Her big roan, ready saddled, was hitched to a post outside, and a moment later she was in the saddle, flying at a hard gallop for Death Valley and reinforcements.

As soon as she had gone, Treherne mounted and rode in the direction of the bunk-house, in order to get the few remaining stockmen. Graves busied himself in getting ready the guns and ammunition, and, by the time Treherne had returned with the three stockmen, he had a regular arsenal laid out on the table. Then they all began to prepare for the expected attack. Binabong homestead had been built years before, when the blacks still existed in that district, and, like all other homesteads of those days, had been provided with heavy wooden shutters against any attack. In the shutters were loopholes, which gave a view of the approach to the house, and on the present occasion they would serve for defensive purposes.

Yvonne, who had hoped and planned for this move on Jameson's part, had, with her usual capacity for detail, seen that the old shutters were in working order. Consequently, it did not take long for Monty and his two companions to close and bolt them. One was left open, in order that Yvonne and the reinforcements might enter, and also that speech could be had with Jameson did he wish to parley.

Then the five men sat down and smoked in silence, as men will who are expecting a hostile attack. Their preparations had taken a little over an hour, and by Monty's reckoning Yvonne ought to have reached Death Valley and be on her way back. It would be a race between her and the Walla-Walla crowd as to which reached Binabong first.

Now and then one of them would rise and inspect the rifles. Then he would return to his seat and run his hand caressingly over his revolver. Beyond that there was no indication that the nerves of each one were strung up to a high pitch.

Of all the things in a situation of that kind, waiting is the hardest even for men who have tasted fire before. With those who have never been in an engagement the suspense of a wait is unnerving until the first shot is fired. Then self is forgotten in the excitement of the moment, and the whole mind is concentrated on the joy of conflict, which is awakened by the pungent smell of powder and the shrill screaming of the shells. In that party Treherne was the only one who had not been under fire. His feelings were somewhat of the above order in consequence, though his mind was also dwelling on the apparent seriousness of his own position.

Monty was the first to descry the approach of anyone, and Graves immediately turned his field-glasses on the distant object in order to see what it was.

"A band of horsemen on the gallop." he announced quietly. "About thirty of them. Yvonne has lost. It is Jameson and his men."

"She may come across from the left." muttered Monty hopefully.

"If she does she will have her work cut out to beat them." replied Graves, still studying the approaching body of horsemen. "They are riding hard, and I can now make out Jameson. He is in the lead, and they are all armed."

"If it wasn't for the danger the missie is running I'd say let 'em come," grunted Monty, twirling the cylinder of his revolver. "I haven't seen the chance of such fun since Bendigo Joe jumped my claim way back in the seventies."

"Unless Jameson's look belies him you will have your wish," drawled Graves. "He certainly hasn't grown any sweeter-natured since we saw him two hours ago."

The oncoming party of horsemen had now reached the home

paddock and were coming on with unslackened speed. In five minutes they would be within hail.

Graves laid aside his glasses and stood close to the window, one hand ready to close the shutter quickly should the necessity arise. Curly had left the room to examine the paddock through a loophole at the rear, in order to see if there were any signs of Yvonne and Gene. He returned just then and reported that she was not in sight.

"All right," answered Graves. "Get ready, boys! Jameson has halted his party and is riding on alone. He evidently intends to speechify again."

They held their weapons loosely and crowded up behind Graves just as Jameson rode to within a few yards of the window and pulled up. For a moment he and Graves eyed one another. Then Jameson spoke, and the quiver of his tones proved how hard it was for him to control himself.

"Who claims to be the owner of this place?" he demanded loudly.

Graves placed one hand over his heart and bowed ironically.

"I am authorised to treat for the owner, Mr. Jameson, What have you to say?"

"I have this to say," shouted Jameson, holding up a sheaf of papers in his hand. "I have here a copy of the mortgage which I hold over the stock previously on this station. I also hold a copy of the mortgage on the station itself, given to me for moneys advanced. In addition to these, of a later date and superseding the mortgages, I hold an unqualified assignment of Binabong Station from one John Treherne to myself.

"Furthermore, I publicly charge the said John Treherne that he, together with other persons at present unknown, did conspire to steal and did steal a number of sheep from Walla-Walla. As true owner of Binabong Station I demand that John Treherne and any others who may be on the property leave peacefully and at once. If this demand is refused I, as owner of the property, will enforce my demand against those who remain in illegal possession.

"And, further, I demand that the said John Treherne deliver himself up peacefully on the charge stated. I make the demand as the rightful owner of Binabong, and also as Justice of the Peace for this district. I give you five minutes to decide. If at the end of that time you refuse to comply with my demands I shall take what measures I deem advisable to evict you by force."

70

"Not bad," drawled the imperturbable Graves. "You ought to run for Parliament, Jameson."

Jameson snorted, but vouchsafed no reply, as he rode rapidly back to his men. Graves once more swept the paddocks in search of Yvonne.

"Nothing doing," he muttered slowly. "Something has delayed her, boys. Close the window. Mr. Jameson is not bluffing. See to your guns. I think we will be getting it warm in a few minutes."

Monty closed the shutter and bolted it. Then he and his two companions took up their posts in other rooms while Graves and Treherne remained to guard the front. At the end of the allotted five minutes Graves applied his eye to the loophole and peered forth. He could see Jameson speaking to his men. Then they spread out in a wide circle, and, at a sharp command, drew their weapons. A moment later the whole party started at a swinging gallop for the house.

"Here they come!" shouted Graves. "Be ready, boys, and, remember, let them fire the first shot!"

At that moment the heavy pounding of hoofs broke on their ears, then came a heavy volley, followed by the heavy plunk of lead as the bullets hit the shutters.

The fight was on.

Tinker gave a shuddor as he gazed at the whitened bones
before him. *(See page 10.)*

Tinker caught wildly at the empty air in a frenzied effort to save himself. His fingers closed convulsively, and with a hoarse croak he plunged over the edge into the abyss beneath.

THE SIXTH CHAPTER.   Tinker's Ghastly Discovery— An Unlucky Fall.

It will be remembered that, when Tinker escaped from the bottom of the wilderness, Gene and his three companions had not lost any time in giving chase. It will also be recalled that they had reached the top of the valley without overtaking him, and that while they halted there Blake had overheard their remarks.

Two theories had been advanced. One was that the lad had heard them coming up the trail, and had sought cover in the scrub which covered the gullies.

The other was that he had never left the bottom, but was still lying low there, waiting for a suitable opportunity to make a safe get-away. The former of those theories was the correct one, and it is just possible that they might have caught the escaping prisoner had not Blake's successful strategy upset their plans.

When Tinker started on a steady lope up the trail he had wisely husbanded his strength. Had he only known of Blake's nearness he would have been saved much suffering, but he did not think it possible that even Blake's methods would discover the secret of Death Valley so soon.

He felt fairly certain of the way, for he had a retentive memory and had kept his eyes open on the way in. If he could once reach the top in safety he knew he had a good chance.

He had covered what seemed a tremendous distance, though in reality it was only about a third of the way, when the sharp ring of hoofs behind told him his pursuers were gaining. He had counted on the necessity for the horses to walk up the trail and on his own ability to keep up a swifter progress, but old Gene had taken advantage of every level bit and was setting a hard pace.

As the sound grew nearer Tinker realised that he must take cover. Still loping he turned into a patch of scrub which stretched up the side of the gully in which he happened to be, and dropped down panting, just as the four horsemen swept by.

Poor Tinker, if he had only known that, at that very moment Blake and Pedro were riding along the gully at the top!

As Gene and his companions passed on Tinker rose and cautiously crept still further into the scrub.

"I'll wait a few minutes," he muttered. "They are bound to go clear to the top, but I can probably manage to get on another stage before they return. When they find I haven't reached there they are sure to post a guard, but I'll have to run my chances of slipping past him. If I remember rightly the scrub is fairly thick there."

With this consoling thought he lay still until his wind returned. Then he rose and made his way, as he thought, back to the trail he had just left. Certainly, it was the bottom of a dead water-course into which he emerged, and, as far as he could see, it was the identical spot where he had entered the scrub.

He started along at a brisk lope, keeping his ears open for sounds of the returning horsemen. For ten minutes he travelled steadily, then, on reaching a bend, he turned round it, and pulled up with a gasp of amazement, to find he had almost plunged headlong over the jagged edge of a sheer cliff.

"Crikey!" he muttered, gazing about him in puzzlement. "How does this occur? I'm hanged if I remember this in the descent!"

He turned and went back round the bend, gazing along the way he had come.

"It certainly looks like the trail," he grunted, "but there is something wrong somewhere. I'll try over to the left. Perhaps the trail goes that way instead of this."

Suiting the action to the word he made his way in the opposite direction. A small, rather well-defined gully opened up, and he breathed easier.

"I am all right now," he thought. "That cliff gave me a shock for a moment."

He again broke into a lope and travelled on quickly until he reached another bend in the gully. This he turned, and suddenly his face went very white.

For the second time he had barely saved himself from plunging over a high cliff into eternity. He slowly retreated around the bend and gazed back down the gully.

"I guess I'm off the trail," he muttered. "The only thing to do is to go back the way I came and keep on until I reach it. I must have passed the turning without noticing it."

He moved at a steady walk back along the gully until he reached the spot where he had struck the first cliff, and from there turned down to the left.

As he walked along he tried to reckon how long he had taken

from the time he had started. One moment he thought it must be about ten minutes, and the next it seemed that he had been twice as long. All the time his eyes kept darting from side to side in search of the trail, he had been walking for several minutes when he saw another gully on his left, and gave a grin of satisfaction.

"That's it," he said aloud. "What an ass I was to miss it, and what precious time I have wasted. I'll have to hustle if I am to make up for it."

Turning into the gully he broke into a run, and for several minutes kept a straight course. Then another bend appeared, and he turned it confidently. If he had been startled at the sight of the cliff on the two previous occasions he was doubly so now at the sight which met his eyes. For the third time he found that he had come out to the face of a cliff, but in this case there was a broad ledge between him and the edge, and on that ledge he saw a sight which made his flesh creep.

Lying in a tumbled heap were two bleached skeletons. Their bony fingers still curled about the handle of a rusty knife, and the twisted attitude of the limbs told their own tale. They had died in mortal combat. When or how was a mystery. That it must have been years before was evident from the whitened condition of the bones.

Tinker gave a shudder of distaste and gazed about him. For the first, time he noticed the opening of a cave which gave on to the ledge, and, for the moment forgetting his own predicament, he approached it. At first his eyes failed to pierce the gloom, for outside the sun was beating down with terrific force.

As his pupils widened, however, he made out what seemed to be a tumbled heap of boxes in one corner of the cave. He struck a match and stepped inside. By the light of the vesta he saw that his first thought was right. There were about twenty boxes piled up against the further wall. They were not large, and Tinker wondered what they could contain.

At that moment the match went out and he lit another. Holding this aloft he approached closer, and put out his free hand to drag one of the boxes around for inspection. His eyes widened in surprise when he found it refused to move, and, dropping the match, he gave both hands to the job. The light from the opening now enabled him to see fairly well. He found that by exerting considerable strength he could lift the box, and this he did. He staggered to the opening of the cave with it and dropped it on the ledge.

"Heavens, that must be full of lead!" he muttered, mopping his brow. "Anyway, I'll investigate it."

Going back into the cave, he lit another match, and began searching amongst a heap of utensils in the corner. He gave a grunt of satisfaction on discovering an old rusty tomahawk, and with this in his hand, returned to the ledge.

Turning his back on those two awful grinning skeletons, he began hammering and prising at the lid. Whoever had nailed it on had meant it to stay, for though the heads of the nails were rusty, they held stubbornly. By dint of perseverance, however, Tinker got it started, and once that had been accomplished, the rest was easy. He tugged and pulled until he got the lid lifted high enough to insert the handle as a lever. Then, with a mighty heave, he strained upwards, and the lid went splintering.

Exactly what he expected to find Tinker couldn't have told. As a matter of fact, he had hardly considered the matter. He knew from the great weight in proportion to the size that the box must contain a very heavy substance, but little did he dream that it was packed with the most precious and almost the heaviest of all metal—pure bar gold.

He sat speechless for several minutes. Were the other boxes packed with gold, and, if so, where on earth had they come from? He was so held in stupefaction that for some time it never occurred to him to examine the other boxes, nor, in fact, to do anything but build a structure of feeble theories. Then his mind came back to earth.

Jumping up, he rushed into the cave, and began straining at the next box on the tier. It was quite as heavy as the last, and, on reaching the ledge with it, he could see it was to all intents and purposes the same as the first one. Again he brought the tomahawk into requisition. He worked feverishly now, all his own troubles forgotten in the excitement of the moment. After some ten minutes' work, he managed to prise off the lid. His expectations were realised to the full. The contents were exactly the same as those in the first box.

"Crikey!" he gasped, squatting down on his heels and lifting out a bar of the precious metal. "Gold—pure gold! There must be four or five thousand pounds' worth in each box. That means in the twenty boxes there is a fortune of eighty or ninety thousand pounds. How, in the name of all that's mysterious, did they get here?"

Mechanically he turned his attention to the two skeletons, taking in the details of those sinister positions which told their own tale. Unconsciously, he was nodding his head slowly and mentally ticking off the suggestions of the attitudes. The twisted limbs, the outstretched right arms, the crumpled up left arms, the pointing of the skeletons head to head, all proved that both had met their fate in a desperate encounter, and did the lad need further proof, there were the knives, caked with a brown rust which was not the rust of water.

Slowly Tinker advanced to the nearest of them, and gingerly drew out the knife from between the bony fingers. He glanced at it closely, and bent lower as he saw two initials cut on the handle. It was with difficulty that he made them out, so old and worn were they, but finally he deciphered the first one a "P." then the second, a "J." Dropping the knife, he stood up.

"Well, by ginger! There was only one notorious individual in this district whose name began with these initials," he muttered. "That was Jackson the bushranger—Peter Jackson. So I guess it's a safe bet that the gold in this cave was Jackson's hoard. But who was the other? Was he one of Jackson's band who wanted a share, or was he some prospector who blundered in here and discovered the hiding-place?"

Tinker was never to know. And yet, sixty years before, when the Indian Mutiny was raging, when Australia was almost totally unexplored, and when gold was still the lure of California, those two men had stood on that narrow ledge and fought their savage fight to the death.

Tinker's conjecture that it was a member of Jackson's band was correct. Thieves had fallen out, and by the mockery of Fate they had both paid the penalty. All those years had that gold lain there undiscovered and untouched. Much good all Jackson's hoarding had done him in the end.

To die by the hand of an enemy, with the curses of his dying opponent ringing in his ears, almost within touch of his treasure, to fall there in the blazing sunshine on that ledge, unwept and unmourned, the helpless victim of the birds of prey who swiftly gathered to the banquet. That had been his end, and still the gold had remained as though in glittering yellow mockery of man's futile efforts.

It was some time before Tinker's thoughts came back to his own situation. When they did he realised that the sun was past the zenith, and that he was hopelessly lost. He had had nothing to eat since the night before, and already the pangs of thirst were beginning to make themselves felt. Was this open tomb to be his own fate? He shuddered as the thought occurred.

Getting to his feet, he went back along the gully still searching for the trail he had missed. On and on he wandered, his every thought now bent on finding his way out. As the maddening thirst increased, he thought of the trickling silver stream at the bottom. The gold attracted him no more. He would gladly have given it all for the privilege of burying his face in that clear stream.

Still the sun kept dropping, and still he stumbled on. He had lost every sense of direction now. All the stories he had heard of Death Valley and its impassable gullies occurred with redoubled force. His throat was parched and dry, and his tongue beginning to swell.

Finally, a mild form of delirium seized him. Time and again he was sure he had found the trail, only to discover that it ended in a yawning chasm. Several times he stumbled and fell, but dragged himself to his feet again and stumbled on. He finally remembered his revolver. Even being a prisoner was preferable to this.

He realised that comparatively few people knew Death Valley, and those few probably had no knowledge of any part of it but the trail to the bottom. If he were to succumb it might be years before his body was found, perhaps never. The thought, sobered him.

He drew his revolver, and emptied every chamber in the air. For some time he listened for a reply, but none came. With a sudden frenzy of rage he hurled the revolver from him. Once again the delirium seized him as he stumbled on.

Finally, on turning a bend, he saw before him the grinning skeletons on the ledge. He had been travelling in a great circle. He gave a dry sob and staggered forward.

As he did so, his foot caught in a small crevice. He caught wildly at the empty air in a frenzied effort to save himself. His fingers closed convulsively, and with a hoarse croak he plunged over the edge into the abyss beneath.

"Oh, pull! pull!" gasped Yvonne. The stockmen needed no second bidding, and foot by foot Blake rose. (See page 85.)

THE SEVENTH CHAPTER.   In Time— Blake as Mediator — Jameson Fooled —The End.

If Blake was startled at seeing Yvonne approaching down the tortuous trail which led to the bottom of Death Valley, he gave no visible sign. At the same time, had a physician placed a clinical thermometer in the hallow of Blake's arm, he would have noticed that the detective's temperature had gone up a point, due, possibly, to the arduous climb.

As for Yvonne, she drew her horse back on his haunches, the action sending a little cascade of stones rolling merrily downwards. Richards, who was leading the way, promptly covered her with his revolver, and the four prisoners growled savagely at him as their horses came to a stop. Blake signed to Richards to lower his revolver; then he stepped forward.

"Good-morning, mademoiselle," he said, smiling ironically.

"Good morning, Mr. Blake," she replied. And though her lips were unsmiling, her eyes glinted softly, and her delicately flushed cheeks told their own tale. "For a Londoner, you seem —er—fairly well acquainted with Death Valley," she added mockingly.

"A charming spot—at the bottom," drawled Blake. "An ideal place for sheep during those dry months. It occurred to me while I was down there that it would be a splendid retreat for, say, stock rustlers."

"Indeed! I am afraid that occupation has died out, hasn't it?"

"Well," answered Blake, wrinkling his brows as though in deep thought, "until very recently I was under that same impression. It seems, however, that I was mistaken. These four gentlemen who look so annoyed, strike me as being a particularly murderous lot; and I greatly fear they have been helping themselves to stock which did not belong to them. In fact, it seems odd that all the sheep I saw at the bottom of the valley bore the brand of Walla-Walla. When I was in Australia before, sheep-stealing was a serious matter. To my knowledge the law regarding it has not been changed."

Yvonne shifted impatiently under Blake's irony.

"Enough," she said, with a click of her white teeth. "Supposing I acknowledge that for the moment you hold the advantage of me. What do you propose doing?"

"My intention, mademoiselle, is to take these four worthy men to

Walla-Walla, and turn them over to the law as represented by Mr. Edward Jameson, who is, I understand, a Justice of the Peace. After that I propose finding out what has become of my lad, Tinker."

Yvonne looked at him with a puzzled glance, which changed to a look of mute inquiry as she turned her gaze to the bound Gene. Gene read her look, and for the first time since he had been made a prisoner, he spoke.

"He escaped, missie," he said gruffly. "We were searching for him when we were outwitted."

"I am surprised that three experienced stockmen, all armed, should be outwitted by one man," she replied, with a hint of sarcasm in her voice.

Gene writhed, but made no reply. Then Yvonne turned back to Blake.

"May I speak with you—privately?" she asked slowly.

Blake nodded.

"Yes, providing the prisoners pass their word not to try any hanky-panky business."

"They will do that," answered Yvonne. "Come, please." she turned and rode a short distance up the trail, followed by Blake. When a bend hid them from view of the others, Yvonne drew up and waited until Blake reached her side. Then she thrust out her small gauntleted hand.

"Won't you shake hands?" she asked naively.

Blake laughed, and, putting out his strong, sunburnt hand, grasped hers.

"Of course. But, mademoiselle, why have you done this? You must know how serious it is."

Yvonne looked at him with a serious expression.

"What are you doing in this affair, Mr. Blake? Are you working professionally?"

"No, not exactly. Jameson sought my assistance, and I gave it— informally."

"Are you stopping at Walla-Walla?"

"No. I am visiting at Mulwana, Campbell's place."

"Ah! It adjoins Walla-Walla. Won't you withdraw from this and let things take their course. Mr. Blake?" she asked, with pleading eyes.

"I am sorry, mademoiselle. It is impossible. Yesterday I might

82

have done so. To-day I cannot. Besides, you yourself have made that impossible by capturing Tinker. By the way, where is he? I must insist on his release, and then, if you are wise, you will surrender peacefully. I will do what I can to persuade Jameson to take no further action."

Yvonne's silvery laugh rang out; then she grew sober, and gazed at Blake in silence for some moments.

"Do you know what is probably happening at this moment?" she finally asked.

"I must confess that I am not clairvoyant."

"In all probability Jameson and his men are besieging Binabong homestead. Jameson threatened to do so a little over an hour ago, and he certainly looked as though he meant it."

"This is serious," replied Blake gravely. "If there is bloodshed it will complicate matters considerably."

"Exactly. I was on my way here to summon help when I met you and discovered that you had arrived first. You have only heard Jameson's side of this argument, Mr. Blake. Do you feel inclined to hear my side of the story?"

"You have never found me unwilling to listen, and then weigh, have you?" he asked gruffly.

"No," she said softly, "never. It won't take long, and I will be as brief as possible."

She bent, forward and laid one hand on the neck of his horse. Then she began speaking in low, rapid tones.

She began with her longing to see Binabong again, and from that went on to the arrival of her uncle and herself. Then she dealt with the haggard owner they had found, and the story of hard luck he had told. Of the assistance he had received from Jameson and the nightly games of chance in which the two men had indulged. Of the loss in this manner of all Treherne's possessions, and her discovery that the cards were marked.

Without pausing, she told him of the idea which had occurred to her, based on her knowledge of Death Valley, and how well her plans had succeeded. Then she told him of her motive, and went into detail regarding the offer to lift the mortgage, and how Treherne, at her insistence, had repudiated the gambling assignment.

Finally, she told of Jameson's call barely an hour before, and of his threats while there.

"So you see," she said, "from my point of view I am in the right, and though my methods have been irregular, it seems to me that conditions justified them."

For some time Blake made no reply. The average observer would have thought that he was inflecting deeply upon the story he had just heard. As a matter of fact, he was not. Impelled by that mental phenomena, the association of ideas, his mind had gone trailing off on an incident entirely alien to the subject in hand.

It had come about through a gesture made by Yvonne as she talked. It stirred some chord of memory, and then he recollected what it suggested. He had seen that gesture before. When or how he could not for the moment remember. His abstracted gaze rested on a single red rose which was thrust in Yvonne's belt, and then he remembered.

It was in London, at the Venetia, after the highly satisfactory ending to that now notorious case, which was popularly culled "The Black Jewel-Case." He and Yvonne had lunched at the grill-room of the Venetia, and it was there that she had worn red roses. It was also there that she had used the quick, grateful gesture which she again used now. Sub-consciously his keen mind was weighing the facts she had presented, but it was not until she laid her hand on his arm that he shook himself free from his reverie.

"I beg your pardon, mademoiselle," he said, flushing faintly. "I am afraid my mind was straying."

"That is not very complimentary to me," she laughed.

"On the contrary," he smiled. "I was thinking of you."

"Then I am indeed flattered." she replied, also flushing.

"Now about this other matter," went on Blake, breaking what threatened to degenerate into an awkward silence. "As I told you, my interest in the affair is strictly of an informal nature. At the same time I felt moderately certain that Jameson must be in the right, although I did not like his suppression of the details regarding his trouble with Treherne. Of course the fact that he used marked cards in order to fleece Treherne, alters the case entirely. As for me, I must say I hardly blame you for your feeling of indignation, although I by no means condone your methods. At the same time, since I am mixed up in this thing, I propose seeing it through, so it seems that once again we are to work as friends, not enemies, mademoiselle."

Yvonne's voice was trembling slightly as she thanked him, and with clasped hands they gazed at each other.

"About Tinker?" said Blake, releasing her hand slowly.

"Truly, I am as mystified regarding his whereabouts as you are, Mr. Blake. He escaped, that is certain, but he may have taken cover in the scrub, or again, he may have reached the top in safety. We can ask Gene."

They rode back together, and found the five horsemen as they had left them. Richards wore a worried look, for he could not understand his rescuer's apparent attitude of friendliness to the leader of the rustlers. He was to wear a much more worried expression, however, when a few moments later, he saw Blake lean forward and release the bonds of the four prisoners.

"I say," he stuttered. "What are you doing that for?"

"For reasons which you wouldn't understand," replied Blake calmly. "Now, Richards, my plans are changed. Toss over your gun, please."

The man looked mutinous, but one look at the steady grey eyes decided him. He passed over his revolver, and sat gloomily waiting for Blake to continue.

"I am not going to make you a prisoner again," went on Blake, "and you will be free to go where you will when we reach the top. I shall take your horse, however, and it will be necessary for you to return home on foot. Have you any objections to that?"

"I don't see what good it would do if I had." growled Richards.

"Not a bit." answered Blake cheerfully. "Now, Gene." he went on, turning to the head stockman. "Where is the lad you captured?"

"Tell him all you can, Gene." broke in Yvonne.

"There ain't much to tell," grunted the stockman, who still felt decidedly ill-tempered over being tricked first by Tinker and then by Blake. "All I know is he got away. I don't know exactly how much start he had, but it couldn't have been over half an hour. I called the others, and we started after him at once. We saw no signs of him on the way to the top, so we left Harris on guard. Then this man took a hand in the game, and played the winning card. If the lad went up the trail he must have managed to get clear. On the other hand, if he took cover in the bottom to watch his chance, well, then he's still there. That is all I know."

Blake nodded thoughtfully.

"H'm," he muttered. "It looks as though he had succeeded in getting clear. In that case he will be making his way on foot across the paddocks."

"I guess that is the case," remarked Gene.

"Then nothing is to be gained by remaining here," went on Blake. "If you are ready, mademoiselle, we will move on and see what developments are taking place at the homestead."

"Then you will help?" asked Yvonne eagerly.

"Of course," answered Blake quietly. "Shall I take the lead?"

"Please."

And as Yvonne's eyes followed his swaying figure up the trail she sighed, and the little demon of hopelessness again stabbed her as she thought what it would be to have him always take the lead for her.

In this fashion the little party again started, with Gene keeping as close a watch on Richards as the latter had previously kept on the stockman. Blake's unhesitating movements showed how well he had studied the trail on the way in, and on reaching the top he signed to Gene to relieve Richards of his horse. When that had been accomplished, and the angry stockman had started on his long walk across the paddocks, Blake turned to Yvonne —

"Are we ready?"

"Yes."

"Then follow me."

He dug his heels into his horse's side and followed by the others, swept away over the stony approach to Death Valley, at a hard gallop. For twenty minutes they rode steadily without drawing rein. At the end of that time, just as they were emerging from a patch of scrub, Gene gave a loud hail, and Blake drew up.

"What is it?" he asked sharply.

"Body of horsemen to the left," grunted Gene laconically. "Might be some of Jameson's men."

Blake looked in the direction indicated, and for some moments studied them in silence.

"I make eleven," he said.

"That is what I make, too," said Yvonne. "I wonder what Jameson's men are doing out there?"

"I don't think they are his men," rejoined Blake, shading his eyes with his hand.

"Unless I am mistaken, that is my host, Campbell. I can recognise him by the white horse he is riding."

"By Jingo! that is right," broke in Gene. "Mr. Campbell always rides a white horse, and I don't know of anyone else in the district who does."

"Then we will ride to meet them," said Blake. "If Jameson has kept his word, their assistance will be of value."

As he spoke, he started off, and in a moment the whole party were riding in the direction of the others. They, in their turn had evidently been seen, for Blake saw the white horse come to a stop, and the others follow suit. As he drew nearer he could distinguish the features of his host, who wore a look of surprise.

"What's up?" he called, as Blake got within earshot.

Blake made no reply until he pulled up beside the other. Then in a few brief words he told Campbell enough to show him how matters stood.

"The point is, old man," he said, when he had finished, "will you come along and help?"

"If the situation is as you say it is, of course I will," answered Campbell. "Though it is a ticklish business mixing up in these bush feuds, and I want to be dead certain where I stand."

"You have my good word for it that the situation is as I have stated it to be." rejoined Blake quietly.

"That's good enough for me, old man. Lead on. We follow."

Blake turned his horse and galloped off, with his augmented party following. Yvonne was riding neck and neck with him, and from time to time, she gazed across at the stern profile which rose and fell so easily to the motion of the horse. Ten minutes' hard riding brought them to a dry creek, and as they gained the further bank, the sound of intermittent firing broke on their ears.

"He has kept his word." called Yvonne. "That sound comes from the direction of the house."

Blake nodded, but did not reply. Instead, he set a harder pace than ever, and as he rode, drew his revolver. The others did the same, and in this fashion they swept into the home paddock. Already could be seen white puffs of smoke issuing from the loopholes in the windows, and from the cover of a small blue-gum plantation could be seen others showing where Jameson's men lay.

Whether it was because both besiegers and defenders saw the approaching body of horsemen, or for some other reason, Blake did not know, but as they drew nearer, the firing stopped. Blake swept on until he was within a hundred yards of the plantation before he drew up. The rest of his party grouped themselves about him, and barely had they done so when Edward Jameson himself broke cover and rode towards them.

On recognising Blake and Campbell he naturally concluded that the new party were friends.

"By thunder! I'm glad you have come," he said, pulling up and mopping his brow, "I've got thirty men, but we haven't been able to—"

He broke off as his eyes rested on Yvonne and her four stockmen.

"What are they doing here?" he asked, with darkening brow.

"They are my prisoners," replied Blake coolly. "But tell me, Mr. Jameson, why are you attacking this place?"

Jameson ponderously drew out the documents which he had read aloud before the attack, and once more read them over.

"Those are my reasons, and as a Justice of the Peace, I am entitled to take the measures I have taken. I gave them warning to vacate the place, and, in addition, demanded the surrender of the stock rustlers. They complied with none of my demands, and as individuals in wrongful possession of my property I am well within my rights by doing what I am."

"Any of your men hit?" asked Blake casually.

"Five of them winged, two seriously."

"Supposing I agree to persuade those in possession to turn the place over to you peacefully, Mr. Jameson, will you call a truce?"

"Certainly."

Blake turned to Yvonne.

"Have I your authority to deal in the matter?"

"Whatever you do I will abide by."

"But I must have Treherne given up!" snarled Jameson.

"If, when we finish, you still insist on that, I promise you he will go without resistance." said Blake. "Now are you satisfied to have me conduct the negotiations?"

Jameson nodded.

"Yes," he said curtly.

"Then I will ask you all to wait here with the exception of mademoiselle. She will come with me."

Together the two rode towards the house, and the opening of a shutter indicated that the defenders had been watching the conference.

Graves stood in the window, a revolver in one hand and a cigarette in the other. He nodded to Blake as the latter rode up.

"Glad to see you!" he drawled. "Friend or foe?"

"Friend," smiled Blake, slipping from the saddle and giving a hand to Yvonne.

They stepped across the verandah, and in through the open window, where Blake was introduced to Treherne. A glance at the latter's haggard but honest eyes told Blake that Yvonne had not been mistaken in her judgment of the man.

"Anyone hurt?" he asked, taking a cigarette which Graves proffered.

Treherne shook his head.

"Not a scratch on one of us."

"They have been potting at us like anything for half an hour," grinned Graves. "I think we got some of them, though."

"You did," said Yvonne. "Five."

"Good enough. They opened fire first, and by thunder they aimed to kill, too. But what is the next move?"

Yvonne explained how she met Blake, and the little surprise he had prepared for Jameson.

"That suits me," said Graves, when she had finished.

"How about you, Treherne?"

"Oh, I'm agreeable," he replied gloomily. "As far as I can see, I am in for it seriously."

"You wait," remarked Blake. "Now, then since you all agree that I conduct matters, I think it would be as well to have Jameson come along."

He moved to the window as he spoke, and beckoned to the owner of Walla-Walla.

"Will you come in, Mr. Jameson?" he called, as Jameson approached. "They have all agreed to my acting for both parties."

Jameson threw the bridle-rein over his horse's head and stamped across the verandah. A moment later he stood scowling amongst them.

"Let us sit down," remarked Blake, in his suavest tones. "There are several points to discuss."

When they were all settled, Blake turned to Jameson.

"Now, Mr. Jameson," he said, "let me get all the facts before I make my suggestions. If I am right, your claims are based on the following points. If I am wrong, you will please correct me."

"To begin with, you loaned Mr. Treherne a considerable sum of money, taking his sheep as security."

"Yes."

"After that, you loaned him further sums, and took a mortgage on Binabong Station."

"Yes."

"Then you received an unconditional assignment of the property from him to you."

"Yes."

"Following this, Mr. Treherne offers to redeem the mortgage."

"Yes."

"This you claim he had no right to do."

"Certainly. He had already assigned the place, and had nothing more to do with it."

"On top of this he sold the place to this lady, and she assumed all liabilities in connection with it."

"Which was illegal, and, of course, void."

"We will discuss that later. You then gave notice that possession must be given to you within a specified time?"

"Yes."

"Failing this, you would take it by force?"

"Yes."

"They refused and, using the assignment as your authority you kept your word?"

"Yes."

"In addition to this, you accuse Mr. Treherne of stealing your sheep and kidnapping your stockman?"

"Yes; and as Justice of the Peace demand his surrender."

"Exactly. Well, I can tell you, Mr. Jameson, that your sheep were taken by the people you suspect, for I have found them!"

"Where are they?" cried Jameson, in amazement; while Treherne looked at Blake as one looks at a traitor. Only Yvonne was smiling.

"They are on this property," replied Blake. "You see, you have in me a good witness. Now, I would like to ask you a question, Mr. Jameson."

"Go ahead, Mr. Blake," he replied, with a self-satisfied smile, feeling that in Blake he had an ally who was worth while.

"For what consideration did Mr. Treherne give you an

unconditional assignment of Binabong?"

"Is that essential?" asked Jameson, shifting uneasily.

"Certainly. Unless I know all the details I cannot referee properly."

"Well, he owed me a lot of money over cards, and I gave him his chance to get square. He accepted, and if he tells the truth, will acknowledge that I was mighty generous in the matter. I offered to release him from all his obligations if he won. If he lost, I was to take the property. You can see that he had decidedly the best of the bargain, for I had already loaned him a big sum on it."

"Your offer was undoubtedly of a very generous nature," said Blake suavely. "I must say that, on the face of it, your case is very strong, Mr. Jameson."

Once more the self-satisfied smile appeared on Jameson's face. The mention of the gambling had been the only awkward point, and he had surmounted it beautifully. Blake rose and leaned against the table with crossed arms.

"Mademoiselle, will you please give me a pad of paper?" he said, turning to Yvonne.

This had been agreed upon by them at Death Valley as Blake's signal to her to smuggle him a few of the marked cards. Yvonne rose at once and left the room. Silence reigned until she returned, bearing the pad of paper. She handed it to Blake, and resumed her seat.

"Now, if you are all agreeable, I am ready to deliver my judgment," said Blake.

One and all agreed silently. Then, lifting the pad in his hand, he began to speak, looking at Jameson.

"My judgment is," he said slowly, "firstly, that all the sheep on Binabong and Walla-Walla be turned over, unconditionally to Edward Jameson. Secondly, that Binabong Station be given up to Edward Jameson, and a proper transfer duly executed. Thirdly, that John Treherne and all others resident on Binabong surrender peacefully to Edward Jameson, to stand their trial for sheep stealing."

As each sentence fell in measured accents from Blake's lips, Jameson nodded his head in satisfaction.

Graves smoked nonchalantly, while Yvonne studied the floor. Treherne had gone white, and was shifting nervously.

"Those are the conditions to be complied with by those resident upon Binabong, providing"—and he paused on the word—

"providing Edward Jameson fulfils the two following conditions: Firstly, that he withdraw his men and uses no further force—"

"Sure!" broke in Jameson, with a grin.

"And secondly, that he satisfies me regarding this."

As he spoke Blake opened the pad of paper and flicked the cards in his fingers. Jameson first looked puzzled, then a deep purple dyed his face.

"I don't understand!" he said thickly.

"These cards," went on Blake, imperturbably, "were the cards used when John Treherne lost his property. On examination they prove to be marked cards, Mr. Jameson, and Mr. Treherne says they were provided by you. What do you say?"

"I say it is a cursed lie!" snarled Jameson.

"I believe you are prepared to swear that you found them in the room shortly after the game was over, mademoiselle?"

Yvonne bent her head.

"And you, Graves?"

"I am."

Blake turned back to Jameson.

"In that case, Mr. Jameson, there is only one thing to do, and that is to take the whole thing into court. There it can be thrashed out, and the question of those marked cards proved."

If each word had been a drop of ice it could not have affected Jameson worse. He gazed at Blake in fascination, realising at last that the detective had been playing with him all the time. He had flattered himself that he had successfully pulled the wool over Blake's eyes, and the latter's whole judgment had seemed entirely in Jameson's favour until the last condition.

Jameson's face changed from purple to blotchy grey, and he glared at Blake speechless with baffled rage. He was beginning to feel the vague clutchings of fear at his heart, and the keen rapier point of deadly meaning behind Blake's calm mask.

"There is no necessity to go into court," Jameson finally managed to articulate. "I hold all that is necessary for me to take possession!"

"Exactly!" replied Blake suavely. "You see, though, as referee in the matter, I must be absolutely fair to both sides. That being so, it is essential for me to consider the question of these cards."

For a moment he held Jameson's gaze; then he went on softly:

"That marked cards were used there seems no doubt. Mr.

Jameson disclaims all knowledge of them. Mr. Treherne does the same. In that case, all I can see is that the matter be taken into court. The use of such cards in any gambling transaction is a most serious matter; but when the transfer of a great property like Binabong rests on it, then there is nothing else to be done."

Jameson made an inarticulate sound, but Blake gave no notice. Instead, he continued more softly and more slowly than ever:

"Of course, in this affair, as in all affairs, there is an alternative. As referee in the matter, I would suggest the careful consideration of it. A lawsuit based on the question of marked cards would be a most odious affair, whichever way it went."

"What is the alternative?" asked Jameson thickly.

"The alternative is a compromise."

"In what way?"

Blake gazed at the floor, and tapped slowly on the table.

"If Mr. Treherne, or whoever is the present owner of Binabong, should offer to repay to Mr. Jameson all moneys borrowed, and if Mr. Jameson accepted this offer, it seems that all claims of justice would be satisfied. In addition, I would suggest that Mr. Treherne hand to Mr. Jameson the pack of marked cards, and in return Mr. Jameson give back to Mr. Treherne the assignment which he holds. In that way all parties are just where they stood before. No one loses by the transaction. Of course, by doing that, Mr. Jameson gives up all claim to Binabong; but perhaps he would prefer such a course to the notoriety attendant upon an unsavoury lawsuit. That, gentlemen, is my suggestion. It is up to you."

Blake drew out a cigarette as he finished speaking, and looked down into Yvonne's smiling eyes. Graves still smoked nonchalantly, while Treherne and Jameson regarded each other cautiously. Finally, Yvonne spoke.

"What is your decision, Mr. Jameson?" she asked sweetly. "Do you feel inclined to hand back the assignment for the cards?"

For answer, Jameson stood up, and with a barely suppressed oath drew out the assignment and dashed it on the table.

"Give me the cards," he muttered chokingly.

Yvonne opened a drawer and took out the balance of the pack. Blake added the few he held, and Jameson seized them viciously. Once they were in his possession he swung on Treherne.

"Curse you! You have schemed cleverly, haven't you?" he

blazed. "I'll give you until to-morrow to take up that mortgage. If you don't do so then, you will hear from me in another way."

"You are addressing the wrong one, Mr. Jameson," broke in Yvonne. "I have already informed you that I am now the owner of Binabong. If you will hand over the documents you hold, you can have the money now. I have it ready."

As she spoke, she again pulled open the drawer, and took out a thick bundle of notes. These she tossed to Blake.

"Will you please act in this as well, Mr. Blake?"

"Certainly, mademoiselle," smiled Blake. "Is this for the loan on the land or for the stock as well?"

"For both."

"What do you say, Jameson? Are you ready?"

Jameson signified that he was, and in five minutes the matter was completed. Only when Yvonne signed her name did he turn and study her closely.

"Cartier?" he muttered absently.

"Why, yes, Mr. Jameson," smiled Yvonne. "I am surprised that you did not recognise me before."

Jameson glared and rose.

"You have beaten me," he said savagely. "But there is a future."

"Exactly." answered Yvonne— "and there are also marked cards. Good-bye, Mr. Jameson; I think your party is growing impatient."

Without, a word Jameson turned, stepped through the window, and stamped heavily across the verandah. A moment later he was galloping towards his men and, as though in final mockery at the plans of man, a black cloud was already rimming the horizon, presaging the coming rain and the breaking of the drought.

The continued non-appearance of Tinker was beginning to make Blake look anxious. As though in answer to his master's thought Pedro, who had returned from Death Valley with Blake, rose from his place under the table and gazed upwards with a look of mute inquiry. Yvonne placed her hand on the big fellow's head and regarded Blake shyly.

"You have been awfully good to me, Mr. Blake," she said softly, "I won't thank you, for I know you would rather I wouldn't."

Blake shrugged.

"You are worried about Tinker, aren't you?" went on Yvonne.

"Yes, I am getting a bit worried."

"You will go in search of him?"

"Yes."

"Will you let me and my men assist you?"

"Gladly."

"What is your plan?"

"I think the best plan will be to take Pedro along, start at the hut where Tinker was a prisoner, and follow his scent from there."

"Of course. That will save time. I will have Gene muster the other men at once."

"Thanks!" said Blake. "In the meantime, I will ask Campbell to join us."

At that moment Campbell himself appeared. A few words from Blake explained how matters stood and, like Yvonne, he insisted upon joining in the hunt.

Ten minutes later every available man was mounted, and with Blake leading the way they swept on at a hard gallop in the direction of Death Valley.

Arriving at the bottom, old Gene went in front, and led the way to where Tinker had been a prisoner. There Blake put Pedro's muzzle to the scent, and the big bloodhound started off strongly. Across through the patches of trees which Tinker had used as cover he went, and on reaching the short gully turned up it and took his way along the trail to the top. Blake's face cleared somewhat as he did so, for if Tinker had reached the top, the chances were he had gone straight to Campbell's place. His brow again wrinkled, however, when Pedro turned into the scrub.

Blake pulled up the dog and dismounted. The others followed suit, and leaving three men in charge of the horses they followed Pedro on foot. Along the trail taken by Tinker he went. At the first precipice Blake drew in his breath sharply, but breathed more easily when Pedro turned and went along to the left. He got another shock when they came out at the edge of the second precipice, but once again Pedro turned back. Yvonne was close to Blake, and as they went along the bottom of a gully she spoke.

"He was confused," she said in low tones.

Blake nodded, but did not speak. He knew those signs only too well. Once in his younger day's he had been lost in the Great Salt Desert, and knew what it was to go wandering about lost in a wild expanse where no man might be met. His eyes were clouded, and his face very grim as he went on. Behind him came the others. Gene and his companions suggested spreading out and sweeping through the scrub, but Blake signed for them not to do so.

Pedro had the scent strong, and would lead them in the right direction more quickly than a hundred men could. Twice they passed the same point, and Blake knew Tinker had begun that most awful of all experiences —travelling in a great circle.

Another hour passed, and still Pedro kept on. Finally, on turning a bend; Blake gave a sharp gasp as he saw the edge of another cliff, and on the ledge before him two whitened skeletons.

Dashing forward he drew up sharply, and gazed in amazement at the two opened boxes of gold which lay before him.

"He has been here," he said steadily. Then raising his voice he shouted: "Tinker! Tinker!"

No answer. Again he shouted, and still no answer. Only the cliffs beyond caught up his voice and threw it back in mocking echoes, the whole vast amphitheatre formed by the cliff's jeering Tinker! Tinker! in an uncanny duplication of Blake's voice.

Those behind had crowded forward at sight of the gold, but Campbell and Yvonne waved them back.

"We don't know what it means," said Yvonne, "but for the present it must wait. The lad is more important."

All this time Pedro was straining on the leash. Gene had dashed into the cave, and came out to report the presence of more boxes, but no sign of the lad. By one accord they avoided the grinning skeletons.

Pedro seemed so anxious to go ahead that Blake eased the leash. His face went strangely white as the bloodhound moved straight to the edge and did not come back.

Instead, he lifted up his voice in a deep bay which sent a chill to the hearts of those who heard it. With a smothered groan, Blake dropped flat and crawled to the edge. It was a thousand foot drop to the bottom of that precipice, and if its face was as sheer as the faces of those surrounding it, then nothing of any description would protrude and serve to break the path.

Sick with the thought, Blake crept outwards and looked down. As he did so his heart gave a great leap and his pulses hammered. His hand shook in a manner strangely unlike him, though what he had seen had been sufficient to make the strongest heart quail. About thirty feet down he saw a small clump of trees which apparently grew from the sheer face of the cliff.

In the midst of their branches he had seen a sprawling figure, and that figure was Tinker's. The branches swayed dangerously with the unaccustomed weight, and it seemed as though every moment must see the lad's body go hurtling into the bleak eternity beneath.

Blake, got slowly to his feet, and with tense features faced the others. He swayed like a drunken man, and spoke thickly.

"Belts, stock-whips, stirrup leathers—quick!" he ordered.

Yvonne, reading his expression, crept to the edge and peered over. She drew back, pressing her hand convulsively to her breast.

"Oh, quick!" she gasped, "He looks as though he might go at any minute!"

With that knack which is the bushman's, every man in the party had ripped off his belt, while half a dozen had followed old Gene back to where the horses had been left. Precious moments passed, but though it seemed they would never come they were in reality less than half an hour.

On their return they lost no time in twisting the pieces together into a strong rope. Then each man volunteered to descend, but Blake waved them back.

"This is my job," he said gruffly.

Slipping one end of the improvised rope under his arms, he stepped to the edge and peered over.

"Hold tight, and lower me slowly," he said. "Watch that it doesn't fray on the edge."

With that he sat down, and while the stockmen strained on the rope he slipped coolly over the edge. Now that he was actually doing something for the lad's release, he was as calm as ever.

Yvonne had again crept to the edge, and as she saw Blake swinging in space above that awful drop all the pent-up love in her heart welled up and fought with her tears for the control of her eyes. Blake glanced up and met her look. His own eyes softened for a moment, then he looked down and signed to Campbell to lower away.

Down, down he went until his feet almost touched the top branches of the tree in which Tinker lay. Lower still he went, until he was on a level with the lad. Then ever so slowly he started swinging until each swing brought him nearer and nearer to the place where Tinker lay. His hands went out cautiously, for one false move might cause the branches to sway and precipitate the lad into the abyss beneath. Then his fingers grazed the lad's shoulder, and the next moment he had gathered all his strength into one great effort.

Yvonne watched in fascination, as he stretched out his arms and grasped the unconscious lad under the shoulders. The tree swayed ominously. The next moment Blake had swung free, gripping Tinker, who dangled beneath him, Blake's hold the only thing between him and eternity.

"Oh, pull, pull!" gasped Yvonne. "He has got him!"

The stockmen needed no second bidding. Slowly and steadily they drew up in order that no undue strain would come on the rope. Foot by foot Blake rose, until his head was on a level with the ledge. Higher he came, then one great heave and he was over. A dozen hands grasped Tinker and drew him over as well, and a mighty cheer rent the air at the success of Blake's truly magnificent rescue.

Yvonne took his hand and, regardless of the presence of the others, held it, the while her whole soul gazed at him from her eyes. Then she released it and, stumbling to her feet, sank down on a box of gold.

Campbell was already busy over Tinker. A swallow of the strong spirit from Campbell's flask caused his lips to quiver and then open. He gazed about him for a moment, dazed. Another swallow sent the blood rushing through his veins, and brought back his recollection. Though still weak he was unharmed.

"I remember now," he muttered. "But how did you get me up?"

Campbell pointed to Blake. Tinker gripped Blake's hand. He was too full of gratitude to speak, but those two understood each other.

A few minutes later, when Tinker had eaten a couple of sandwiches, he began to tell them his experiences, which dealt with his finding of the gold and culminated in his sudden plunge over the edge of the cliff.

It was a very excited party which carried out the other boxes and opened them. Blake judged the quantity in each box to be less than Tinker had estimated. He put it at three thousand pounds, but, even so, that gave a total of sixty thousand. Truly a magnificent hoard to find.

When the last box had been opened and the last gaze satisfied, when the strange find had been discussed from every point, and the knives had received their due share of attention, the stockmen shouldered the boxes, and the whole party made their way back to where the horses stood. Pedro kept very close to Tinker, and in some strange, canine way seemed fully aware of the terrible situation in which his young master had been.

It was at the close of a very eventful day that they reached Binabong. On the way it was decided to report the find of gold to the authorities. Yvonne insisted on Tinker taking the full percentage as the finder, but the lad stubbornly refused to do anything else but divide whatever he got with her, so at that they left it.

The cloud on the horizon was now a huge black stretch which was slowly creeping across the heavens. Treherne's eyes filled with hope as he watched it, for Yvonne had offered him the managership of Binabong on a half-share basis—an offer which he gladly accepted. Gene and Yvonne's other stockmen departed to bring back all the Binabong stock from Walla-Walla, and Campbell with his men had gone home, Tinker going with them. Graves had gone to his room, and only Blake and Yvonne remained. She followed him outside when he went to get his horse, and as he sprang into the saddle she laid her head against the horse's shoulder.

"Are you leaving soon?" she whispered.

"Yes, I will go to Melbourne to-morrow," answered Blake gently.

"Then—then I won't see you again?"

He shook his head slowly.

"Not out here."

"It is good-bye, then?"

"Yes."

She straightened up wearily, and stood for a moment with bent head. Then she lifted his hand, and for one brief moment laid it against her warm lips.

Releasing it, she turned and stumbled blindly back to the house, while Blake, with a deep sigh and misty eyes, dug his boots into his horse and, with Pedro following, rode away across the paddocks, his hand still burning from the touch of her lips, and his mind still thinking of the look in her eyes when he was dangling over the abyss.

THE END.

[35700 WORDS]

OTHER CONTENT INCLUDES 'THE "U.J." "IRON WALLS OF GREAT BRITAIN" GALLERY'; ONE SEGMENT OF THE SERIAL 'THE TRAGEDY OF THE OKLAHOMA' BY CECIL HAYTER; 'CASSELTON'S LITTLE CHAT'; AND 'A WORD FROM THE SKIPPER'.

An Amusing Letter from a Public-School Boy Reader.

I say, you chaps, you know young Thomkins, the silly idiot who thinks he knows everything? Well, he's gone right off his rocker now. Of course, that in itself doesn't really matter much, only, you see, his particular form of madness directly affects me, and that is serious. Of course, he is an ass, we know that, but that isn't any excuse for his thinking he can go one better than me in photography.

It's no use trying to talk to Thomkins when he gets on his high horse, I keep on yelling at him that he doesn't stand a chance with me up against him. Why, the Skipper was going to illustrate an article with one of my photographs once, but at the last minute he found he hadn't room for it. I should have won first prize in a recent competition if some silly ass hadn't sent a better one than me. At least, the Editor said it was best. But then, what does the Editor know about it? And the worst of it is, these editors have got such beastly side. When you offer to assist them in the judging they simply freeze you.

But to get on to that ass Thomkins. He's so lucky with his photographs. For consummate luck— I don't know what consummate means, but they say it in books—he collars the whole bunshop. He generally manages to get his photographs out of the toning-bath just at the right time.

That is what is worrying me. I'm generally so unlucky.

I either get mine too deep or not deep enough. Of course, it's all a matter of luck. But I've got a ripping photograph up my sleeve; got it on my— But you wait and see. It will be described when it's published in THE UNION JACK.

You know, some people never can tell when they have gone far enough. Masters generally seem to forget that they have all been boys themselves. Sauce, I call it. The latest order to the prefects is to stop all "dormi" feeds.

I can't understand masters. How would they get on if there were no boys to teach? Fine old hole they would he in, and this is their appreciation. So I thought out a ripping joke. Young Hazel minor is a bit of an electrician in his way, so I asked him if he had got some electric batteries. Well, after a lot of jaw he said he had got about six 4-volt accumulators and about twenty lamps. Then I told him my idea.

Next, we told everybody all over the Form that we were going to have a feed in the dormitory that night. We also made quite sure that the prefects got to hear of it. It worked rippingly. That night, when we went to bed we had some plates and things, the six accumulators, and each boy had a lamp, with the wires all connected. When we got in bed Hazel put the gas out and turned the electric lights on, and when we put the lamps into our mouths the sight was awful. Then we rattled the plates and things just as if we were feeding.

Immediately in rushed six or seven prefects. But they didn't get far. Old Hadley gave a howl of terror and fled.

Just as the others were going to bolt that ass James burst out laughing, and they— Well, it was worth it, anyhow!

I gave old Thomkins a fright the other day. I got a piece of soap and traced lines all over his large full-length mirror— I forget what they are called— and, of course, the reflection in the glass made them look like cracks. When Thomkins went into the room he thought his mirror was smashed; and the way he went on when he found it was a joke—well, some people haven't any idea of a joke.—

Yours, CASSELTON.

A Word From the Skipper

Fair, open, and honest criticism is what I ask of you. It helps me to keep the "UNION JACK" essentially a paper for all classes. I value equally, criticism from the highest to the lowest.

NEXT WEEK'S SPECIAL CHRISTMAS DOUBLE NUMBER.

I have had so much to say about next week's special feast, my chums, that I feel I cannot say much more.

I can only emphasise what I have already told you, viz:

IT WILL BE TOP-NOTCH !

Do not miss it yourself, and do not allow anybody you know to miss it.

THIS WEEK'S SPECIAL AUSTRALIAN NUMBER.

For a long, long time my Australian chums have been clamouring for a number containing a yarn of Blake in Australia, and at last they have got it!

This issue in many respects is going to make history. For one thing, it shows how I really do try to give my readers just the stuff they want.

And all I ask in return is for them to do a little talking on my account. That they will do this I feel certain.

This is a most ideal opportunity for beating up new chums for me. I want all my Australian chums to introduce this issue of the "Union Jack " Library in every place possible. In other words, GIVE THE OLD PAPER A GOOD LEG UP!

It will NOT be labour in vain.

A FEW LETTERS FROM AUSTRALIA.

"Wanagyl,

"Gippsland,

"Victoria.

"October 18th, 1913.

"Dear Skipper,—Just a line or two in appreciation of the Union JACK. *I have been reading it some seven years now, and I wouldn't miss it for anything, and I always order in advance. The Yvonne yarns are my favourites; then Wu Ling comes next. Glad to hear you are giving us another double number. I am anxiously awaiting it, to see which side Yvonne takes. I would like to have an all Australian yarn, and one in which Blake comes across a clue to Tinker's parentage, and finds out who he really is. This last would be much appreciated by all your readers. As I have never seen any letters from Australia, especially Gippsland, I would like to see this in the Chat, but I won't be disappointed if I don't. Wishing you and your paper every success,*

"I am,

"Yours sincerely,

"Harry G. O'BRIEN. "

"Creighton.

"October 17th, 1913.

"The Skipper,

"Dear Sir,—I received your letter, and was very glad to think I had someone to write to in London. As for the books, I have not received them yet, but when I do get them I will be very glad to distribute them amongst my chums.

"Well, dear Skipper, I have got you two more new readers, and they say they like the Yvonne yarns the best. I read "Yvonne's Last Revenge,' and am looking forward to your double number, as you say Yvonne appears in it.

"Well, dear Skipper, I think I will draw to a close, wishing you and your good old UNION JACK *the greatest success, and waiting to hear from you again.*

"I am,

"Yours faithfully,

"V. CHEGWEDDEN. *"*

"Rose Street,

"Glenelg,

"South Australia.

"August 25th, 1913.

"Dear Skipper,—Having seen the various letters sent to you by chums from different parts of the Empire, we thought we would send a few lines to you, telling you what two, at least, Australians think of your stories. The UNION JACK *is available in this State every Thursday, and if you don't secure your copy on that day, you have to go without that week. This will show you that there are 'a few' who read the 'U. J.'*

We personally prefer the Yvonne v. S. B. stories. We both enjoy these yarns very much, and when we have finished reading them, they are passed on to some of our chums, who enjoy them as much as we do.

"Don't you think you could send S. B. to Adelaide one of these days?

"Another suggestion. Don't you think S. B. and Yvonne could get married? We don't think it would make any difference to Tinker, because it would be several years before a Blake Junior would come on the scene to take Tinker's place, and by that time Tinker would

have a business of his own, because he can't always be dependent upon 'his guv'nor.' Hoping you will consider these suggestions.
    "We remain,
    "Yours sincerely,

"M. C. G.
"G. L. G."

A YEAR OF GREAT EVENTS.

The year 1913 might well be termed the year of tragedy, but intermingled with its horrors are many happenings of world-wide importance, happenings that will go down through the years in history, and which will in all probability make history.

The new oil-fuel battleships have a great future before them, and the first oil-driven cruiser has now been launched. Fifteen-inch guns are an established fact, new and more powerful torpedoes are to be used, and now our Naval authorities have been experimenting with a new power.

The new power, which is called the "F" rays, is an invisible force of concentrated electrical rays. It will, it is claimed, explode explosives at a great distance, and to test the truth of this statement, a mine, heavily charged, was placed under the hull of the light cruiser Terpsichore, some feet below the water-line. The rays were then turned on the vessel from a distance —not known—and the mine exploded with such force as to so badly damage the ship's bottom that she was in a sinking condition. The utmost secrecy was maintained, and only the bare facts given above are obtainable, but the experiment was pronounced to be highly satisfactory.

If this power is all that it is claimed to be, it will revolutionise warfare. Its effects can well be imagined, and terrible would be the destruction it would deal out should the occasion ever arise for it to be used.

And, lastly, the Panama Canal is open, and only needs clearing before it is navigable. And there is still another month to run. We wonder, are any more sensations awaiting us?

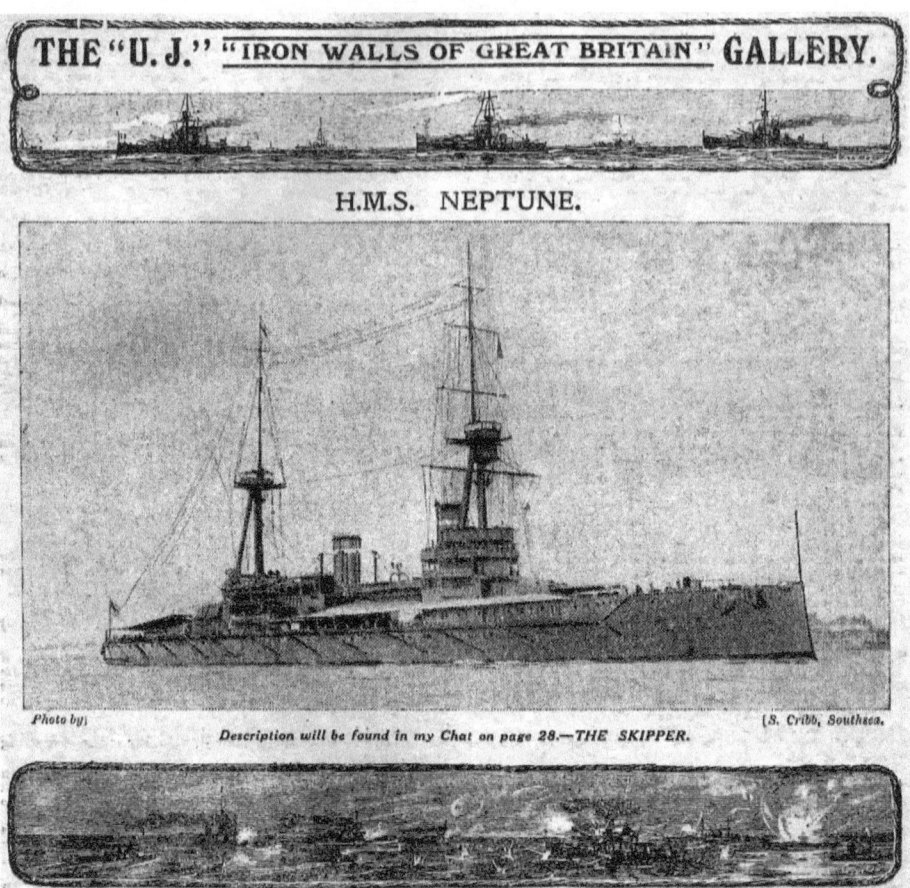

H.M.S. NEPTUNE.

Photo by: [*S. Cribb, Southsea.*

Description will be found in my Chat on page 28.—THE SKIPPER.

H.M.S. NEPTUNE. *(See page* 23.)

This battleship is of an earlier type than those whose photographs I have already published. She was completed in 1911, and does not mount the 13-in. guns, but 10 12-in. and 16 4-in. Her displacement is 19,900 tons, and her speed 21 knots.

A WORD TO WALES.

I should like to express my very sincere sympathy with those of my Welsh chums who have suffered loss in the terrible mine disaster at Senghenydd, and also my admiration of those who so nobly risked their lives in attempting to rescue their fellow-men.

THE SKIPPER.

You can put this down to "Spooner" if you like, when you tell it. The bird and joint appeared on the banquet board at the same moment, and the nervous curate, who was to carve, said to the pretty girl who sat next him: "Miss Moody, will you have dutton or muck?" And then he wanted the ground to open up and swallow him.